Fame School

Rivals!

Cindy Jefferies

USBORNE

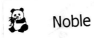

Noble

Thanks to Seb for all the drumming tips,
and to David White and Lindsey North
for so much else.

For Paul, always.

First published in 2005 by Usborne Publishing Ltd., Usborne House,
83-85 Saffron Hill, London EC1N 8RT, England. www.usborne.com

A CIP catalogue record for this book is available from the British Library.

JFMAMJJASO D/07

ISBN 9780746061190

Printed in Great Britain.

Glamour! * Talent!

* Stardom! *

* Fame and fortune *
could be one step away!

Welcome to

Fame School

For another fix of

read

1 Cymbals and Drums

"Can you grab that door?"

Danny James was struggling to carry his bass drum safely into the Rock Department. He didn't have any proper drum cases, and protecting his instrument was vital.

Ed Henderson, Danny's friend and roommate, leaped up and held the door open while Danny brought the drum into the room and put it down.

"D'you want a hand with the rest?" Ed asked.

Danny nodded gratefully.

"Thanks. And Happy New Year, Ed."

The two boys made their way along the corridor and outside, where the rest of Danny's kit was waiting to be

Rivals!

carried in. It was the first time Danny had managed to bring his drum kit to school. Most people brought their own instruments with them to Rockley Park, the brilliant boarding school where aspiring singers, songwriters and musicians went. But Danny's mum didn't have a car, and it was difficult enough getting Danny to the school. Luckily, this time he had managed to get a lift with someone his mum knew, who had a van big enough to take Danny and his drums.

Until now, Danny had needed to use the school's drum kit. That was fine, but everyone set up their instruments slightly differently, so it would be good to have his kit here, and leave it arranged just as he liked. He would be assigned a small practice room to keep it in, but for now he needed it in the Rock Department for a jam session in the morning.

Ed looked at the remaining four drums and the collection of cymbal stands and cymbals in the open plastic boxes that were waiting to be moved. "Why couldn't you learn the guitar like me?" he teased. "It's much easier to move about."

Cymbals and Drums

Danny laughed. "But your huge amplifier weighs a ton!" he protested.

"True," Ed admitted. "And I got a great effects box for Christmas, so that's something else to lug around. Thank goodness my voice doesn't need any equipment to make it work."

"Danny! Hi, Ed!" It was Chloe, bursting in like a whirlwind. Like Danny, she was a scholarship student and they had been at their last school together. Unlike the boys, who both wanted to be rock stars, she intended to be a pop singer.

"Isn't it great to be back?" she said excitedly. "Wow! Are these your drums? I haven't seen them before. They must have totally filled your bedroom at home! Do you need some help?"

"Yeah!" said Ed before Danny could reply. "Can you hold the doors open while we get this lot in?"

"Thanks!" Danny added. "That would be great."

With Chloe's help it didn't take too much longer to carry all the equipment into the Rock Department. Danny looked at the heap and sighed.

"I wish I could afford some cases," he said. "The kit would be much safer, and easier to move."

"Never mind," said Ed. "It's in now. All you have to do is set it up."

Chloe laughed. "I wouldn't know where to start," she said. "And where are you going to put it?"

Danny followed her gaze around the room. "There's either here by the door, or that corner," he said pointing across the room. "I think just here will be fine though. It's only until after the jam session."

"What's this for?" asked Chloe, holding up a shiny silver rod, bent at a strange angle.

"It's one of the legs from my floor tom. Look, there are two more. You slot them in like this."

"I'll go and sort out my guitar, if you're okay now, Danny," said Ed.

Danny looked up. Ed was obviously itching to get his guitar and amp ready for the morning. "Yeah, thanks," he said, and Ed headed over to his own equipment.

Things were hotting up in the room. Guitars and

amps, cables and microphones were everywhere, and there was lots of excited conversation. Then, Judge Jim Henson, Head of Rock, came in. One by one, everyone stopped what they were doing and fell silent.

"Welcome back!" he said. "It's good to see you all settin' up so enthusiastically. There's another socket behind that curtain," he reminded Ed, who was holding the plug to his amp. "I'll be in my office if you need me," he added, picking his way across the room to the other door.

Everyone respected Judge Jim. He was the most senior teacher at Rockley Park and had played guitar with some of the most famous names in the music business. His dreadlocks were grey, and he was old enough to be Danny's grandfather, but making music was his life, and he inspired his students like no one else.

"It's just as well there are only two drummers in the lower school," said Chloe. "I don't think there would be room for any more! Look, there's Tara. I must say hello and then I'd better get out of everyone's way."

Rivals!

Danny gave Chloe's roommate a wave, and went back to assembling his kit. He'd bought it second-hand, and it wasn't the best kit in the world, but he was very fond of it. At home, he had to play it with special sound-damping pads, so he didn't disturb the neighbours. Now he was looking forward to hearing what it could really do. He had all sorts of plans to buy better cymbals for it, but cymbals were terribly expensive, and he would have to save a lot of birthday and Christmas money before he could do that. In the meantime, he had a new pair of drumsticks, really good ones that his mum had given him for Christmas, and that was a start.

Danny fixed the bass pedal and arranged the rest of the drums in front of his drum stool. His cymbals lay in an old, plastic crate, protected between pieces of blanket he'd begged from his mum. He quickly put their stands up, and fixed his favourite cymbal, a crash, onto its stand. He was fixing the ride cymbal when the door burst open.

Charlie Owen thrust his way into the room with his

Cymbals and Drums

arms round a large drum case. Two smaller cases were balanced on top and a heavy cymbal bag was swinging from one hand.

"Charlie Owen is in the building!" he announced as he advanced into the room.

"Careful," warned several people as he wheeled round. But Charlie couldn't see properly from behind his pile of cases and, in spite of Danny's added yell, he backed right into the cymbal on its stand.

There was a crash, and the cymbal fell over.

Just in time, another of Danny's roommates, Ben Peters, grabbed Charlie and stopped him from falling right onto the rest of Danny's drum kit.

"Cheers, Ben," said Charlie, putting his cases and cymbal bag down in front of Danny's kit. "Sorry about that," he added, turning to Danny. When he saw Danny's drum kit, a smile crept over his face and then he whistled, long and low.

"Is this all *yours*?" he asked. He waved his hand, taking in the drums, cymbals, and the collection of scruffy boxes that Danny was unpacking them from.

Rivals!

"Yeah," said Danny, picking his cymbal back up and checking it anxiously. Thankfully, it seemed to be all right.

"Did you get it in a Christmas cracker?" Charlie asked, picking up one of Danny's stands and fiddling with it.

"Don't do that," Danny told him crossly. "That stand's a bit wonky. You have to fix it just right."

"I bet you do," Charlie agreed, handing it back. "You could do with some heavy-duty stands like mine," he added. "My dad uses ones like I've got when he tours with his band. They're fantastic. Have you got any Zildjian cymbals?" he went on.

Danny shook his head. "No," he admitted.

"My parents bought me a set of hand-finished ones for Christmas," Charlie told him. "*And* I've got a huge ride cymbal now. In fact, I don't know why you bothered to bring your old kit, Danny. You'll never hear it when *I'm* playing!"

Danny watched as Charlie carried his belongings over to the other side of the room and started to take the drums out of their tough, protective cases. He was trying not to let it get to him, but Charlie's boasting had taken the edge off Danny's pleasure in having his own kit here. He looked back at his cheap cymbals and sighed, his happiness gone. He hoped he wouldn't regret bringing his drum kit to school.

2 Jam Session

The next morning, Danny longed to head straight over to the Rock Department, but he couldn't. Although Rockley Park was a school for people who wanted to be pop and rock musicians, it also taught all the normal school lessons. So Danny and his friends had to endure maths, French and science before they could gather for the first rock session of the term.

Everyone especially enjoyed Judge Jim's sessions at the beginning of term. They gave the students their first chance to play together since the holidays, and Judge Jim used them to take note of how much work his students had put in while they were away.

Danny's year had experienced their first jam session

last term, and it had been a very hesitant affair. But this term, everyone knew each other and what was expected of them, so it would be great fun. Danny, at least, had been looking forward to the session since they'd broken up for Christmas.

"I've been practising rim shots," he told Ed. "They're really tricky."

"I spent ages over Christmas trying out different sounds on guitar with my new effects box," Ed said. "I nearly drove my parents mad!"

When they arrived at the large practice room, Tara was already plugged in and warming up with some simple blues on her bass guitar. Ed went over to Ben, who was tuning his guitar. Danny gave him a wave and slid behind his kit. He sat down, and picked up the sticks from where he'd left them on his snare drum.

He looked round the room with pleasure. In spite of Charlie sitting behind his expensive kit and giving him a superior look, Danny felt really lucky to be here, surrounded by other musicians. Most were guitarists, but a couple of people played sax, one played keyboard, and of course there was him and Charlie on drums.

Ed plugged his guitar into his amp and joined in, picking out a tune above Tara's bass notes.

Danny began with some gentle taps on his high-hat, and Tara nodded approvingly. It took quite a lot to make Tara smile, but Danny could see she was really enjoying herself.

The next one to join in was Charlie, but instead of starting quietly like everyone else, he started thrashing his kit, in a different rhythm, totally drowning out the others.

Danny stopped playing and sighed. Charlie was such a show-off. Tara put her bass down, came over to Danny and scowled.

"This is supposed to be a jam session, not a Charlie Owen appreciation society!" she shouted over the racket.

Ed and Ben were stepping up their volume, willing to take Charlie on, and Harry Richards was giving it all he'd got on the sax, but Judge Jim was clapping his hands for silence. Slowly, everyone stopped playing and listened.

"Thank you, everyone," said Judge Jim. "And you, Charlie," he added, as Charlie Owen was last to be quiet. Several people laughed, and Harry, one of Charlie's friends, slapped him on the back.

"I liked that riff you were playin', Ed," Judge Jim went on. "Let's pick that up and run with it...see where it takes us." He picked up a battered old guitar and nodded to Ed, who blushed with pleasure and played the high, whining notes again, while Judge Jim improvised around them. Danny smiled to himself and resumed his gentle drumming. Slowly, everyone else joined in, playing their own improvisations around Ed's. Danny glanced over at Charlie, who was managing to restrain his enthusiasm well enough to blend in. His drum kit looked fantastic with its red sparkle finish, and Danny had to admit it sounded great too. *Never mind,* he told himself. *It's how well you play that matters.*

The next part of the session was the most nerve wracking. Once everyone was comfortable with playing together, Judge Jim would nod at each player in turn. At his nod, they had to improvise a short solo, keeping to the rhythm of the piece.

Ed was first, and then Harry. Next, Judge Jim nodded at Danny, and he took up the rhythm while everyone else listened. Danny was afraid that his kit wouldn't sound too good, but he was pleasantly surprised at the excellent tone of his old drums. It had been a good idea to save up as he had, and put better skins on them. Danny was determined to show off his rim shots too, and he managed three before Judge Jim smiled at him and nodded at Tara to take over.

Next, it was Charlie's turn. For Charlie, he was being quite restrained. Danny listened carefully and had to acknowledge to himself that Charlie's cymbals sounded a lot better than his. It seemed you could get away with inexpensive drum shells, but Danny's cheap, machine-pressed cymbals would never sound as great as the best, hand-finished instruments. It was just a shame that Charlie's rather ragged playing wasn't making the best of them.

Once everyone had played a solo, Judge Jim took the lead on his guitar and brought the session to a loud and triumphant close.

"Yeah, well done," Judge Jim told them. "I can see most of you have put in some good work over the holiday. Danny, can you do another of those excellent rim shots of yours?" he asked.

Danny looked up in surprise. He took a deep breath, aimed carefully at his snare drum and hit a perfect rim shot.

"How long did you practise to get those right?"

Danny shrugged. "Quite a long time," he admitted.

Judge Jim nodded. "It's really tricky to hit the skin and the rim of a drum at the same time. It's a real advanced skill. I'm impressed, and I'm sure your drum teacher will be too." Danny blushed. It was great to be praised on the first day of term. But Judge Jim hadn't quite finished. "There's a lot of volume comin' from our other kit," he continued, looking at Charlie. "But to jam successfully, you need to pay attention to what everyone else is doing."

Rivals!

Charlie grinned, but he looked embarrassed and annoyed.

"Okay, everyone," Judge Jim said. "Lunchtime. Don't forget to unplug your amps, you guitarists, and everyone needs to check the noticeboard for times of their individual lessons."

In the dining room, Danny met up with the rest of his friends. Marmalade, a dancer and his other roommate, had saved places for the Rock Department group, so Danny, Tara, Ed and Ben grabbed their lunch and sat down with the others.

"How'd it go?" asked Marmalade.

"Really well," said Danny. "Great fun."

"*And* he got specially praised by Judge Jim," said Tara. "Teacher's pet!"

"Pay no attention to her," advised Lolly, one of the famous Lowther twins, who were here to expand their careers from modelling into the music industry.

"Everyone knows how hard you work," added Pop, her twin.

"If *I* was a teacher's pet, what sort of animal would

I be?" asked Marmalade, his wild ginger hair flopping.

Danny looked at his friend with a grin. "A yeti," he said.

"Unfair!" Marmalade protested with a laugh. "I'm a much better dancer than any yeti!"

"Chocolate pudding all round?" asked Chloe, getting up.

"I'll help," offered Danny.

Charlie was at the serving hatch with his friend Harry.

"Here's Danny 'perfect' James," Charlie mocked. "With the useless drum kit. How's that wonky stand?"

"Okay," Danny mumbled, filling his tray with bowls of chocolate pudding.

"What was all that about?" asked Chloe as they made their way back to their table. "What's wrong with your drum kit?"

"It's all right," Danny told her. "It's just not as good as his. But I don't think Charlie liked Judge Jim hinting that he hadn't done any work over the holiday."

"Well, you shouldn't be so good," advised Tara, helping herself from the tray. "You showed him up."

Rivals!

"I can't help that," Danny protested. "It's not my fault if Charlie hasn't done any practice." He took a bowl for himself and pushed the others towards Pop and Lolly.

Before he could start his pudding, Tara muttered, "Charlie alert." Sure enough, Charlie and Harry were coming towards them. They pushed behind Danny's chair and Charlie gave Danny a shove. While Danny was trying not to fall off the chair, Charlie sprinkled something over Danny's pudding.

"Oi!" said Marmalade. "What are you doing?"

"Giving him a prize for being so clever," said Charlie with a grin, before he and Harry disappeared out of the dining room.

"What is it?" asked Chloe, peering into Danny's bowl. Marmalade dipped his spoon into the bowl and took a small bit of pudding. It was covered with tiny, white grains.

"It might be poisonous!" warned Pop anxiously, but Marmalade only hesitated for a second.

"Even Charlie Owen isn't that stupid," he told her

before tasting the grains with his tongue. "Salt!" he said, grimacing. "What a mean trick."

"It'll be all right," Danny said, taking the bowl. "I can probably scrape the top off."

But the pudding was completely ruined, and when Lolly went to get him another, they'd all gone. Everyone offered him bits of their puddings, but Danny refused.

"I was almost full anyway," he insisted mildly, though privately he was really annoyed with Charlie. Danny had never had any enemies before. But now, due to no fault of his own, he'd got on the wrong side of Charlie Owen.

"He'll get over it," he said hopefully to Marmalade when they were on the way to history. "Charlie may not be exactly my sort of person, but we were friendly enough last term. He'll soon remember that it's more fun getting on with the only other drummer in the lower school, rather than falling out with him. Look how Ed spends hours discussing guitars and you have all your dancer friends, but Charlie and I have only got each other to talk drumming with."

"Well, if he doesn't stop being stupid soon, you'll

Rivals!

have to take up dancing and spend your time with my lot," teased Marmalade.

"No way!" laughed Danny. "No, I expect it'll be okay. Charlie will soon get fed up with annoying me. He likes having someone to boast to about his drum kit, so surely he can't do that *and* be horrible at the same time?"

3 Drummer in Demand

For the next few days, Charlie left Danny in peace. Everyone was busy getting back into school life, and soon it was as if they'd never been away.

In assembly, Mrs. Sharkey, the Principal, reminded everyone to sort out what they were going to perform at the first concert, due to be held just before half-term.

"I realize half-term seems a long way away at the moment," she said. "But it will come sooner than you think. You will all be assessed on your concert performances, so you need to plan now."

After assembly, Danny was just about to head off for lessons with the rest of the class when Rosie Masters pushed her way towards him through the crush.

Rivals!

"Danny! Wait a moment."

Danny waited. Rosie was a couple of years older than him, and was a seriously good pianist. Danny had never spoken to her before.

"I wondered if you'd like to collaborate with me on a piece I'm doing for the lower-school dancers?" she asked. "It's for the half-term concert."

Danny stared at her. "Really? Why me?"

Rosie didn't play rock music, and Danny couldn't imagine why she wanted him to play with her.

"Mr. Penardos, the dance teacher, is using a piece I wrote called *Rifle Shot*," Rosie told him. "But it needs drums, and Judge Jim suggested I ask you to accompany me because you can play rim shots so well."

"It's true!" butted in Marmalade. "We *are* doing a dance called *Rifle Shot*. It's really sad. I'm an African boy soldier who gets killed at the end. Go on, Danny. Say yes. It'll be cool if you play for us!"

"Well...yes. Of course!" said Danny, feeling very pleased. It might not be rock music, but it would be interesting playing for Marmalade's dance, and it was a great compliment to be asked. How cool to be recommended by Judge Jim Henson!

But Charlie Owen didn't see it that way. "You sad act," he said, once Rosie had gone. "Is that the best you can do for a concert piece? Playing with Rosie Posy for the sweet dancers? Call yourself a rock drummer?"

"We're allowed to perform more than one piece at the concert," Danny retorted. "I've been thinking about playing a solo as well."

"Just as well," Charlie laughed. "Because no rocker is going to want to play with you after they've seen you onstage with Rosie. She's *so* uncool. Hey, Tara!" he added. "Fancy playing bass for me and Harry at the concert?"

Tara wrinkled her nose. "No way," she told him. "Ed and I were going to ask you, Danny. You will play with us, won't you? I expect Ben will be on lead guitar, and Ed will play rhythm."

Danny hesitated. He had somehow assumed that he, Ed, Ben and Tara would get together to form a band for the concert, because they all played well together. But if Charlie wanted Tara to play with him, perhaps it would be mean of Danny to monopolize her. After all, he was committed to play for Rosie now, and he wanted to do a solo as well.

"Um...well, I'd love to, but why don't you play with Charlie for a change?" Danny suggested. "You could even do one song with him and another with me!" he added with sudden inspiration. Tara shook her head.

"I'm doing a solo already," she told him. "And I don't want to do three pieces. You might be able to manage three, Danny, but it's too much for me. I'd rather play twice really well, than three times and make mistakes. Go on. Don't be mean. Say you'll play with us."

"But what about Charlie?" asked Danny in a worried voice.

Charlie glared at him, flushing angrily. "I don't need you to sort out who I play with, Danny James," he said. "I'm quite capable of finding my own band members, thank you."

He gave Tara a long, hard look. "Your loss, Tara," he said, before pushing past her.

Tara snorted. "Oh, very scary," she scoffed. "As if I would worry about not playing with Charlie and Harry. I'd rather play with good musicians than big egos. Why did you try to make me play with him?" she added to Danny. "Don't you *want* to be in a band with me?"

Danny frowned. "No, that's not it," he protested. "It's just that Charlie looked a bit upset when you turned him down, and Rosie had already asked me to play with her. It seemed mean for me to say yes to both of you."

"If Charlie was a better drummer he'd get more offers," Tara pointed out. "But I think he's too lazy to practise properly."

"He *is* a good drummer when he stops boasting and gets on with it," Danny said.

"Well, I don't need you to tell me who to play with, and neither does Charlie," Tara snapped. She dropped back to speak to the twins and Danny groaned.

"I seem to be upsetting everyone today," he told Marmalade.

Rivals!

"Oh, you know Tara," said Marmalade. "She's moody, but she doesn't hold a grudge. She'll be okay."

"What about Charlie?" Danny said. "I've annoyed him again, just when I was making an effort to get on with him a bit better."

Marmalade shrugged. "It's not *your* fault," he said. "But if I were you, I should keep out of his way for a while."

4 Jealousy

It wasn't easy to keep away from Charlie. After all, they were both in the same year, and had all the usual lessons together. Charlie did seem to be bearing a bit of a grudge, and although Danny tried his best to appear unfazed by Charlie's actions, they were beginning to get him down.

"You've got to *do* something," Chloe told him, after Charlie had tripped him up in the corridor and jogged his arm at supper so he spilled hot chocolate all down his jeans.

"He'll stop," said Danny hopefully. "If I don't let him see that it's getting to me, he'll give up eventually."

But Charlie didn't give up. And what was worse, his

Rivals!

best mate started to make life difficult for Danny too. Charlie's friend was trouble. Harry Richards was head and shoulders above Danny, and pretty solidly built too. When he and Charlie knocked into Danny, accidentally on purpose, Danny fell hard against the wall and bruised his shoulder. That night it took a while for him to find a comfortable way to sleep.

At least I can still drum, even if it is painful, he told himself as he turned over carefully in bed. A bruised shoulder would get better, and Danny wasn't one to make a fuss. But over the next few days, however many times he hoped Charlie had got tired of throwing his weight around, he was always disappointed.

"Where are *you* off to then?" Charlie asked, meeting Danny in the corridor the next morning. Danny's heart dropped. Marmalade and the others had been quicker to change after games than him, and so he was on his own. The corridor was usually full of people at lesson changeover time, but unluckily for Danny, now there wasn't a soul about. Danny fixed his face into what he hoped was a confident expression.

Jealousy

"History, like you," he said pleasantly.

"Nah. I've got to miss history. It's my drum lesson," Charlie said.

Danny tried to get past, but Charlie blocked the way. It was obvious that he was looking for trouble.

"You won't need these in history, will you?" he said. Before Danny could react, Charlie had lunged at the bag on his shoulder and grabbed the drumsticks that were poking out. "Nice!" he said, looking at the sticks appreciatively. "Can I borrow them?"

Danny hesitated. Charlie didn't need to borrow sticks from him. He had loads of them, and plenty of money to buy more. But money was tight in Danny's family, and these were the only decent drumsticks he had.

Charlie was smirking. And he didn't seem to expect an answer from Danny.

"I'll just give them a go," he said, grinning widely. Danny tried not to wince as Charlie whacked them against the wall, but they were made of oak, and didn't break.

"Oh dear!" Charlie said, smiling brightly at Danny.

Rivals!

"Is this one chipped? What do you think?" he asked Harry Richards, who'd just dawdled up and joined them.

"It looks a bit broken to me," Harry agreed obligingly.

"Come on, Charlie. Stop mucking about and give them back," Danny said, trying to stay calm. If he showed how anxious he was for his sticks it might make Charlie's behaviour worse. But Charlie didn't need any encouragement. And now Danny was seriously alarmed.

"Don't do that!" he yelled. But it was no good. Charlie was bending down and leaning the stick up against the wall. Danny tried to retrieve it but Harry held him back. Charlie's heavy shoe came down hard on the stick several times and eventually Danny heard it crack.

"What a shame," Charlie said. "Still, one's no good on its own, is it?"

With Harry in the way, there was nothing Danny could do, and even the best drumsticks couldn't withstand Charlie's treatment. As soon as he'd broken them both, he and Harry left Danny and strolled up the corridor together as if their consciences were completely clear.

Jealousy

When Danny arrived in class, his friends could see that something was wrong.

"What happened to you?" asked Marmalade. "I thought you'd catch us up, but you've been ages."

In answer, Danny pulled a piece of drumstick out of his pocket and laid it on the table. Marmalade's eyes widened in disbelief. "That's not one of your new drumsticks, is it?"

Chloe picked up the jagged splinter of wood.

"What happened?" she asked.

Danny yanked the other pieces out of his pocket. He was really upset.

"My best sticks. Japanese oak. They're supposed to last ages. Mum got them for me for Christmas, but she can't afford to keep on buying me stuff." He picked up the two halves of one of the snapped sticks and looked at them hopelessly. "Charlie and Harry ambushed me on my way here. There was nothing I could do."

"Right! That's it," said Chloe firmly. "You have to tell a member of staff. You can't carry on like this. Charlie has been making your life a misery and now he and Harry are breaking your stuff as well. It's just not on."

"Chloe's right," Marmalade agreed. "However jealous Charlie is of you he shouldn't behave like this. Go to the staff room and see someone. Right now. I'll come with you if you like."

"And say what?" Danny asked bitterly. "Please sir, two nasty boys broke my drumsticks?"

"Why not?" Chloe reasoned. "They *are* nasty and they *did* break your sticks."

Danny gave her a small smile. "Charlie isn't going to stop because he gets a telling-off once or twice," he said.

"Danny's right," said Ed, who'd been quiet up until now. "He never knows when to stop, whether it's mucking around in class, or drowning out everyone with his drums. And some of the other kids think he's great, just because his dad's in a successful band and he can get them all sorts of promotional stuff from tours. If Danny complains about Charlie to the teachers, it could make things worse, not better."

"The whole thing's stupid," said Chloe. "He poked fun at you because Rosie asked you to play, and yet he's jealous because she didn't ask *him*!"

"It's nice to be asked though," Ed told her. "And Danny was recommended by Judge Jim. I think that's what he's most jealous of. And Tara turning him down didn't help."

"Don't blame *me*," said Tara, leaning over and poking the broken sticks with her finger. "It's all your fault, Danny. If you weren't so good, I wouldn't have turned Charlie down." Tara really knew how to make a compliment sound like an insult.

"What are you going to do about your drumsticks?" asked Marmalade.

"I've still got my old ones," Danny said. "They're a bit ragged, but they should be all right for a while longer. If they break, I suppose I'll have to ask my drum teacher for more, and get him to send the bill to Mum," he added dolefully.

"Charlie shouldn't be allowed to get away with it," Chloe grumbled. "But if you really aren't going to report

Rivals!

him, we ought to at least watch out for you a bit, so he can't do anything else horrible."

"Good idea," agreed Marmalade. "We'll be your bodyguards and stick to you like limpets. Charlie won't bother you with all of us around!"

5 Protecting Danny

For the rest of the day, Marmalade, Ed and Ben followed Danny wherever he went. It was fine having bodyguards during lessons. After all, he was used to them all moving from room to room together. But by the time they'd accompanied him in and out of the loo a couple of times, and back to his room to collect his spare drumsticks, Danny was beginning to feel a bit crowded.

He'd got the practice room booked for after tea, and when they all piled in there together, Danny knew he was going to have to say something.

"It's not that I don't appreciate your help," he tried to explain awkwardly. "But I don't think I could concentrate on my drumming with you all here."

"I know what you mean," said Ed. "I'm the same when I'm practising my guitar. I hate anyone else listening when I'm trying out new stuff."

"Perhaps we ought to stick around outside then," suggested Marmalade. "Just in case."

"Charlie's always in the telly room at this time of day," Ed reminded them.

"That's true," Danny agreed. "Don't worry, I'll be fine. I don't think anyone else has this room booked tonight, so I might be here for ages anyway."

"We'll swing round later then, just to make sure you're okay," Marmalade offered.

"All right. Thanks."

Danny spent a few minutes adjusting the drum kit, and then started off with a piece he was learning. After running through it a few times, he practised some rim shots.

You had to get the stick at just the right angle so that it hit the snare drum skin and the rim of the drum at exactly the same moment, and although he was quite good at them now, Danny was determined not to let the dancers down during the performance. Timing and accuracy were everything, if Danny was to make those rim shots sound like gunfire at just the right moment in the dance.

At one point, something made him glance up. He thought he caught sight of Charlie's face leering at him through the small round window in the door of the soundproofed room. Danny shivered. Charlie was really getting to him. As if it wasn't bad enough being picked on by him, now he was *imagining* seeing him too! He began to wonder if it had been a good idea to send his friends away after all.

Danny was so unsettled he very nearly stopped his practice and went to find them. Giving in to his fears wasn't something Danny was used to doing though, and he wasn't about to start now. *Don't be such a wimp,* he told himself. *You were going to play along to that CD. Don't let Charlie Owen spoil your fun.*

He'd practised hard and now it was time to relax. So he set aside his anxiety, reached into his pocket,

Rivals!

and pulled out a CD of one of his favourite bands. He put the CD into the practice room's player, and turned up the sound as loud as it would go.

He waited, sticks poised as the final chords of the first song died away. Then it was his all-time favourite. For a few minutes, Danny James *was* the band's phenomenal drummer. He was there, onstage, wearing the wild bandana and weird tattoos.

The pace was amazing. Danny stumbled over some of the fills, and lost his way several times, but by the end of the song he was getting better. The drummer's technique was almost within reach. If only he could speed up a bit more. He replayed the song. Better. Then he played along to the intro to the next song.

He was so immersed in the music that he forgot all about Charlie Owen. Time ceased to matter too, as he worked his way through the entire CD. When it finally finished, he was hot and exhausted, but very happy. It would take him a long time to be as good as his favourite drummer, but every now and then he'd felt what it was like to get it right, to know it was perfect.

He sat back on the stool and arched his back. He'd forgotten all about his sore shoulder while he'd been drumming, but now it was aching again. He really ought to go and have a bath to loosen up his muscles.

He checked his hands. A blister was coming and he had a small nick where the crash cymbal had caught his little finger. If he'd thought he was going to play all the way through the CD, he'd have brought his drumming gloves with him. Never mind. It had been worth it. He'd had a great session.

It must be late. A glance at the clock on the wall told him that it was bedtime. No time for a bath then! He'd have to hurry back to the boys' house or he'd get told off.

He slipped the CD back into his pocket and buried his sticks deep inside his bag. Charlie would be in his room by now, and no threat, but there was no point in Danny taking chances with his possessions again. Even though these sticks were pretty worn, they were his last pair. From now on, his precious drumsticks would stay with him at all times, and firmly out of sight.

Rivals!

Danny slung his bag over his shoulder and went to the door. He turned the handle, but the door remained shut. He grunted with surprise. All the practice room doors were self-closing, but their springs weren't *that* strong. He gripped the handle again and turned it firmly. The door shifted slightly but still didn't open. It must be jammed somehow. Danny heaved at the door, but it still refused to open.

"This is ridiculous," he muttered. "What's the matter with the stupid thing?" He tried again and again, but the door stubbornly refused to budge. He peered through the little round window into the corridor, but no one was about. Then a much older boy came out of another practice room, a little way down the corridor.

"Hey!" Danny yelled to the retreating back of the boy. "Hey! Help! I'm stuck!" He banged the door with his fist, but the boy couldn't hear any sound coming from the soundproofed room.

Danny groaned. Where were his friends? They were supposed to have come back here. Why hadn't they turned up? What had gone wrong? There was no way they'd be allowed out of the boarding house at this time of night.

I could play again, until someone comes, he thought. But, for the first time in his life, Danny didn't want to play the drums. He didn't like being trapped. It made him uneasy. What if, for some reason, he wasn't missed and had to spend the night here? It was a soundproofed room. How airproof was it? Would there be enough air to last the night? He'd already used up loads while he'd been drumming.

He went and got the drum stool and put it close to the door. That way he could keep an eye out for people and sit down at the same time. But he watched for ages, and no one was around. It would soon be time for the *older* pupils to go to bed!

There was no way of getting out and no way of getting help. It didn't do to think of the worst, but Danny's mind kept running away with him. What could he do, for instance, if a fire broke out?

6 An Unlikely Rescuer

Danny had almost given up hope of *ever* getting out of the practice room, when he saw a figure coming his way. He waved frantically, but the person was still too far away to notice him in the small window. Danny waited, in an agony of suspense.

"Please let him come to this end of the corridor," he begged under his breath.

It was Dave Fallon, the Head of Maintenance at Rockley Park. Had someone sent him to rescue Danny? Mr. Fallon was in charge of the estate gang, who did everything from cutting the acres of grass to unblocking sinks. Now, he was striding purposefully towards Danny's room. Danny waved, shouted and banged on the door, and at last Mr. Fallon noticed him. He looked very startled to see someone there. He hurried up to the door and bent down by the door handle.

Danny couldn't see what Mr. Fallon was doing. Whatever had jammed the door was taking an age to fix. But eventually he stood up again. In a second, the door was open and Danny was free.

"Thank you!" said Danny gratefully. "The door was stuck and I—"

But Dave Fallon was scowling. "Who did this?" he demanded, holding up a long piece of electric cable. "What's been going on?"

"I don't know," said Danny truthfully.

"Well, some idiot had got you stuck in there good and proper. This cable had been tied round and round the door handle and then onto that hook in the wall. Couldn't call it knots. The cable was in a right mess. More like a poor attempt at knitting! Some of your mates mucking about, was it?"

Danny shrugged, but inside he was seething. It was just the sort of stupid trick Charlie would play. He hadn't *imagined* seeing the other drummer after all. Charlie really *had* been leering at Danny through the window.

"I'll take the hook off," Mr. Fallon went on. "It's not needed, and it'll stop this happening again." He looked at Danny and shook his head. "You lot. I don't know... Flipping kids!" Putting down a CD he had been carrying, he pulled a screwdriver out of his pocket. "Blast! The screws are all painted up."

Danny's bag was still in the room, and he didn't want to leave without it, but he couldn't get past the struggling maintenance man.

"That's better!" Mr. Fallon straightened up and pocketed his screwdriver and the offending hook, while Danny took the opportunity to retrieve his bag. "Go on, then. Hop it!" the maintenance man said. "Isn't it past your bedtime?"

To Danny's surprise, Mr. Fallon disappeared into the practice room and closed the door firmly behind him.

I thought he must've been sent to rescue me but he hadn't at all, Danny told himself, as he hurried away. *Mr. Fallon was coming to the practice room anyway.*

An Unlikely Rescuer

He had an Elvis Presley CD with him too. How odd.
But Danny couldn't afford to waste time thinking about
the maintenance man. He had to get to his room as
quickly as possible and hope that Mr. South, his
housemaster, wouldn't notice him sneaking in.

He was in luck. It was bedtime for the older boys in
the junior house, and Mr. South was busy checking
that they were getting ready before he came back to
the juniors to turn their lights out. Danny raced along
the passage and into the bathroom. He didn't bother
to wash, but gave his teeth a swift brush. In their room,
Marmalade, Ed and Ben were all waiting for him.

"Thank goodness!" Marmalade said, sitting up in
bed. "Are you okay?"

"Charlie must have tied the door up and I couldn't
get out," Danny told them as he scrambled into his
pyjamas and fell into bed. "What happened to you lot?
I thought you were going to come back to check
up on me?"

"We came over here to play pool and forgot about
the time," Marmalade admitted sheepishly. "We were

going to fetch you when we remembered, but Mr. South saw us and said it was too late to go back into school."

"Marmalade did try to sneak out, but old Southy caught him and sent him up to bed," explained Ed. "And Charlie has been here for ages, so we thought you must have just forgotten about the time. We were just going to tell Mr. South that we were worried about you."

"I suppose Charlie is all tucked up in bed," Danny said angrily. "Well, I think I'll go and have a word with him."

Before anyone could stop him, Danny got back out of bed and headed down the corridor to the room Charlie shared with Harry and a couple of other boys.

"I've had it with you, Charlie Owen!" Danny said from the doorway. "Just lay off, will you?"

"What do you mean?" asked Charlie, trying without much success to look aggrieved. "What have I done?"

"You know very well," Danny replied. "You tied up the door of the practice room so I couldn't get out."

"Not me," Charlie protested, smirking at Danny.

"I wouldn't dare to do such a thing to our precious star drummer."

"You did!" snarled Danny furiously.

"Prove it!" Charlie laughed. "I've been here for ages. Ask anyone."

Harry grinned at Danny from his bed on the other side of the room. "It's true," he said. "We've been watching telly all night."

Danny was fuming, but he knew he couldn't prove that it had been Charlie who'd tied up the door, and without proof he could do nothing.

"I'll get you for this," he threatened.

"Nah, you won't," Charlie replied, settling his head calmly onto his pillow, ready for sleep. "You don't have the guts."

Danny picked up a stray slipper from the floor, and was just about to hurl it at Charlie when a voice came from behind him.

"Lights out, Danny. Stop mucking about and get back to your room." It was Mr. South.

Charlie's smirking face made Danny's blood boil,

but there was nothing he could do with Mr. South waiting for him. Danny turned and made his way reluctantly back to bed. He liked Mr. South, and if he'd had any proof that Charlie had tied up the practice room door he'd probably have complained to the housemaster about it. But with lack of proof there was no point, just like the incident with his drumsticks. Charlie would simply deny everything. It was so unfair.

Once Mr. South had switched off their light and gone away, Marmalade tried to cheer his friend up.

"You didn't get into trouble for being late, so Charlie's trick didn't work," he said. "Don't let him make you lose your temper. He's not worth it. How did you escape from the practice room anyway?" Marmalade asked.

"Dave Fallon saw me and let me out."

"What was *he* doing there? It's a bit late for him to be working, isn't it?"

"I don't think he was on duty," Danny said, remembering the CD. "I think he must have come to use a practice room. He had an Elvis Presley CD with him."

"Perhaps he's a secret Elvis impersonator!" Ed said. "What a laugh!"

"Well, whatever he is, it was lucky for me he came along when he did," said Danny, turning over in bed. "And Mr. Fallon has fixed the door so Charlie won't be able to play that trick on me again."

"Good!" said Marmalade. "Perhaps Charlie will give up annoying you now... There isn't a lot else he can do."

"I hope not," said Danny with feeling.

7 Disaster!

In spite of the problems with Charlie, Danny practised hard on his piece for the dancers, and at the end of that week Mr. Penardos, the dance teacher, said they could do a run-through with Danny and Rosie Masters. Almost everyone in the lower school who wasn't involved went along to watch. Even the recording engineer, Mr. Timms, who usually spent most of his time in the studio, turned up. Danny was very pleased when he noticed him, in his thick glasses and trademark grey cardigan, sitting near the front. He admired Mr. Timms and was glad of an opportunity to impress him.

Marmalade and the rest of the dancers took their places onstage, while Danny settled onto his stool behind the drums. He'd set his kit up earlier that day, so he knew it was just as he liked it. He ran his fingers lightly over the drums and cymbals to double-check they were the right distance away from him. Then he raised his sticks.

With a nod from Rosie on the piano, he began with a haunting African beat. The dancers came slowly alive to the insistent sound. Rosie echoed Danny's rhythm on the piano, and introduced the first hints of the tune.

Danny was concentrating really hard. This wasn't his usual furious but accurate pounding of the drums. It was nothing like rock music. In this piece, he had to be very controlled and measured. In another few beats he would play the small tom-toms fixed to his bass drum, and then he'd bring in the cymbals.

As soon as he hit the tom he knew something was wrong. It swung away from him, swivelling on its stand. Danny didn't pause in his playing, and somehow managed to bring it back towards him. But then the other tom did the same and he knew he was in trouble.

Rivals!

What's happened? he thought in a panic. *Should I stop?*

But he couldn't bear to stop. Marmalade and the other dancers were doing really well. If he made them stop while he sorted the kit out, he'd ruin everything.

Danny always set up his kit carefully. Before any performance he checked and re-checked that the drums and cymbals were properly tightened onto their stands. He knew the kit had been fine when he'd looked at it earlier. But as he hit the splash cymbal he could feel it sink down, could see the legs of its stand splaying out wider and wider. The cymbal was sinking, sliding down until it came to rest right on top of his floor tom.

The drum kit had been sabotaged! That was the only explanation. For a moment, Danny had worried that his ancient cymbal stand was the culprit. But *everything* was loose, not just the one dodgy fixing. And there was nothing Danny could do about it.

Desperately he tried to play more gently, but the music was supposed to get louder, not quieter. If his kit

would only hold together until the dance was over…
Another ten bars and it would be the vital rim shots.

Come on, Danny urged himself. *You can do it.*

Surely his beloved drum kit wouldn't let him down?
But even Danny couldn't play well now. The bass drum
pedal was loose, the cymbals were sinking and the
drums sounded terrible because the skins had been
slackened so much. Danny gritted his teeth and tried
to carry on, but with the very next beat the whole kit
collapsed!

The noise was awful. The cymbals crashed off their
stands and rolled amongst the dancers. They sounded
like a heap of dropped saucepans! Marmalade tripped
on a cymbal and almost fell. Then the floor tom leaned
drunkenly to one side and toppled with a resounding
thump, sending the splash cymbal spinning across the
floor until it disappeared over the side of the stage and
landed with a crash at Mr. Penardos's feet. Even the
little snare drum collapsed on its stand with a buzzing
rattle. Danny was left sitting in a mess of tangled silver
stands and the ruins of his drums.

Rivals!

It looked more like a heap of wire coat hangers and discarded hatboxes than his precious drum kit. Danny's friends looked horrified, but Charlie and Harry burst into loud honks of laughter. They stopped abruptly as Mr. Penardos leaped onstage, holding the cymbal. He looked absolutely furious. "An' do you think this is a funny joke, my friend?"

Danny shook his head, blushing scarlet with embarrassment and anger at being made to look so stupid.

"Get this mess cleared up. We will manage without you today. No' you, Marmalade. Stay with the rest of the dancers until we can restart." He handed Danny the cymbal and waited, his arms folded impatiently.

There was an awkward silence, while Ed and Ben helped Danny collect his kit together and pile it swiftly out of the way. Rosie smiled at Danny sympathetically, but nothing could lessen his embarrassment.

As soon as the restarted dance had come to its conclusion, and the dancers had left the stage, Danny and his friends collected all the drums, cymbals and

Disaster!

stands, and carried them back to the practice room.

"Even the drums' skins have been loosened!" Danny fumed. "*And* I checked it all just before break. It's going to take me *ages* to put it all right."

"It must have been Charlie," Ed said.

"But I don't have any proof," growled Danny. "Again!"

"Calm down," Marmalade urged him. "We'll guard your kit too from now on."

But Danny was beside himself with fury. "That's it," he snarled. "No more. He's not getting away with it. I'm definitely going to get him for this!"

"Don't let him see that he's upset you," Marmalade warned him as they went in for lunch. "It'll only encourage him to do something worse. At least nothing got damaged."

Charlie was loitering by the serving hatch, watching them line up.

"You were a 'crashing' success with the dancers," he jibed as they drew close.

For a moment, it seemed as if Danny hadn't heard.

Rivals!

He looked at Charlie vaguely but didn't reply. Then, as if he'd noticed the drink in his hand for the first time, he brought it up, level with his eyes. He'd never retaliated before, and Charlie could have had no idea what he was about to do. But slowly, with grim pleasure, Danny raised the glass higher, and poured the contents all over Charlie's head.

For a stunned moment Charlie stood there, his hair dripping with sticky orange juice. The juice was running into the neck of his shirt, as well as down his nose, and onto the floor.

"Oi!" yelled one of the kitchen staff. "Mop that up!" But Danny had already taken his tray and was sitting quietly at a table nearby, taking no notice of the uproar at the serving hatch.

Charlie shook his head and several girls squealed as sticky drops flew in all directions. Someone from the kitchen thrust a cloth and mop at him. He grudgingly cleared up the worst of the spill and wiped his face several times. But he couldn't eat lunch like that. He'd have to go and wash his hair, and change out of his sticky clothes. None of his friends was prepared to forgo their lunch to go with him. So Charlie made his way out of the dining room alone.

"Loser," Danny muttered in satisfaction as he watched him go.

8 A Summons

After lunch it was English, but before the lesson began the teacher had something to say.

"I've just had a message for Danny and Charlie," she said. "Judge Jim Henson wants to see you both, straight after lessons this afternoon. Now, let's get on. Today we're going to look at the lyrics you wrote for homework, and see how you did."

Danny couldn't concentrate. What could Judge Jim want with both of them? Had Charlie complained about the orange juice in his hair? If so, Danny would have plenty to complain about too. But he still worried about not being able to prove any of it. Several people had seen Danny tip the juice over Charlie's head, but Danny still had no proof of any of Charlie's misdemeanors.

He gave Charlie a sideways glance, but his enemy's expression was unreadable. For once, he was getting on with his work quietly. Did that mean he was worrying about Judge Jim too, or was he confident that Danny was going to get into trouble while he would not?

The whole afternoon was an agony for Danny. He quite liked English, especially when it was connected to music, like today, but even learning about writing song lyrics didn't help his concentration now.

"I don't *think* I've done anything wrong," he said to Ed on the way to French. "Apart from at lunchtime, I mean."

"Perhaps it's nothing to do with you and Charlie falling out," suggested Marmalade.

But Danny was still worried. "I can't imagine it could be about anything else *except* that," he said gloomily.

At last the afternoon's lessons were over. Instead of going into tea with his friends, Danny went straight to the Rock Department and Judge Jim's study. He met

Rivals!

Charlie outside and they went in together. Danny wasn't in any sort of mood to speak to Charlie, and Charlie was looking everywhere but in Danny's direction.

They walked through the main room, where they had enjoyed the jam session at the beginning of term. It was silent now, although there were plenty of guitars waiting for their owners to plug in and make music.

Judge Jim's study was at the end of a short corridor. For a moment they both hesitated, and then Danny took a deep breath, went up to the door and knocked.

"Yeah?"

Judge Jim's unmistakable, deep voice rang out and Danny opened the door.

The room was a clutter of paperwork, CDs, photographs, spare leads and guitars of various types and ages. In a pottery bowl on his desk was a collection of plectrums, pencil stubs, gaffer tape – which had a million and one uses – and several jack plugs belonging to long-abandoned leads. Judge Jim was sitting on the edge of his desk, tuning a Flying V guitar, but he put it down and stood up when the boys came in.

"Well?" said Judge Jim, as he went round to the far side of his desk and sat down in an old wooden armchair with a faded, patchwork cushion. "What d'you want to tell me?"

Danny hesitated. He hadn't expected that. What *did* he want to tell the man he respected more than any other in the world? There was a lot he *could* say, but he wasn't sure Judge Jim would be impressed if he started bleating about the horrible things Charlie had done recently.

Charlie was silent too, his head was down, and he was concentrating on rubbing the toe of his trainer along the thick carpet on the floor. Danny was determined not to behave as if he was guilty of something. He looked at Judge Jim and cleared his throat.

"Well?" Judge Jim was looking at him, with one eyebrow raised into his grey dreadlocks.

"We're having a few problems," Danny told him.

It sounded feeble, but Judge Jim was nodding his

head seriously. "I'd go along with that," he agreed, "from what I've been hearin'."

Charlie entered the conversation in a rush. "He's always bragging about how good he is. He steals my band members and he doesn't give me a chance."

Danny was so surprised his mouth fell open. But Judge Jim seemed to be taking Charlie seriously.

"And what's your complaint about Charlie, Danny?"

Danny shrugged. Whatever he said, Charlie would deny it, and Danny had no proof. "I'm sorry if Charlie thinks I've been bragging," he said. "I didn't think I was. But we're not getting on too well at the moment. I wish we were," he added more firmly. "I just want to get on with the music."

"You think you're so clever—" started Charlie.

"Quiet!" Judge Jim's voice wasn't loud, but the authority in it made Charlie shut up at once.

"Quit complainin' and get on with workin'," he told him. "Then you won't need to complain any more. And," he added to Danny, "no one likes a wise guy, so make sure you're not one. You need all the friends you can get in this business. Don't throw them away, however troublesome they might be." He hesitated, and Danny thought he caught a flicker of sympathy in the old man's eyes.

"You both came to this school because you convinced us you were serious about your music," he continued. "But it looks like you've forgotten about that." He stared hard at Charlie, until Charlie mumbled something and looked away.

"And when I start to get complaints about my students lettin' down other departments, I get very annoyed," Judge Jim said.

Danny's heart sank. Mr. Penardos must have told Judge Jim about the disastrous rehearsal. Danny could accuse Charlie of sabotaging his kit, but he had a feeling that accusations were the last thing Judge Jim wanted to hear.

"You have to learn to get on," Judge Jim said, "whatever your differences. Don't let them get between you and your music." He stood up and walked round to the front of his desk, where he perched on the corner and retrieved the guitar he'd been tuning.

"And, as you don't seem capable of organizing yourselves for the concert without complainin', I'll do it for you."

Charlie's head came up and he seemed about to say something, but Judge Jim cut him off.

"You will both choose a solo piece," he told them. "And Danny, you'll play *Rifle Shot*, with a properly set-up kit," he added dryly. "You, Charlie, will play with Tara and Harry. Choose whatever song you like, but it must be a proper collaboration, not you tryin' to boss everyone around."

Danny caught his breath. Tara would be furious. And what about Ed and Ben? But Judge Jim hadn't finished.

"Several famous drummers have played duets together very successfully," he told them. He picked up some pieces of manuscript paper from his desk and held them out. "This is called *Conversation Piece.* Go away and learn it. And then practise it. *Together*."

"But..."

Judge Jim glared at Charlie. "But nothin'. You'd better learn to get on together, because you'll be playing *Conversation Piece* at the half-term concert, and I want it to be perfect."

9 A Dreadful Night

That evening, when lessons were over and Danny was in his bedroom, he took a closer look at the drum music Judge Jim had given them. His heart sank. It would be a wonderful piece for two friends to play. If they got the timing right, the to and fro of drums being played sometimes in turn and sometimes together would give a real sense of the instruments talking to each other.

Judge Jim had been right. It would take close collaboration to make it perfect. Danny couldn't see how he'd ever get Charlie to work closely with him, but he didn't want Judge Jim to think *he* was the one being uncooperative. He sighed heavily and pushed the music to one side.

A Dreadful Night

Ed came in from the bathroom, towelling his hair vigorously. "Cheer up," he said, discarding the towel and joining Danny. "It can't be that bad."

"It's worse," replied Danny gloomily. "I can't see how Charlie and I will ever be ready to perform this at the concert. We're supposed to be alternating all the time. Look. This is his line of music and underneath is mine. His snare starts off and then mine comes in. Then it's his toms and then mine, and so on. If we don't play properly it'll sound terrible!" Danny ran his fingers along both parts of the piece.

Ed looked, and gave a low whistle. "I see what you mean." He pointed at a place further along in the music. "I can't read drum music that well, but even I can see you're going to have to get the timing really sharp for it to sound any good. I suppose Judge Jim thought it would force you to get together."

"I know," agreed Danny miserably. "And I did try to discuss it with Charlie after tea, but he just didn't want to know." Danny cleared away the music and tried to forget his worries for the moment. He just had time for

Rivals!

a few pages of the book he was reading. It would be lights out in a few minutes.

Marmalade came in with Ben. He closed the door and leaned against it.

"Pillow fight!" he announced dramatically.

Danny looked up from his book. He wasn't in the mood for pillow fights. He was too miserable. "Count me out," he said.

"You can't count yourself out," Marmalade protested. "It's not my idea. I just overheard Charlie in the bathroom. His room is going to take on our room after lights out. You won't be able to lie there and ignore it!"

The discussion had to stop, because Mr. South arrived to turn their lights off. For a few minutes after he'd gone they all lay quietly in the dark. Then Marmalade sat up and switched his bedside light back on.

"As soon as they reckon it's safe they'll be in here," he whispered hoarsely. "What are we going to do?"

Danny felt his misery turn to anger at Charlie. If it wasn't enough that Charlie kept picking on him and refused to discuss the piece they had been told to play, now he was going to start a pillow fight between their rooms, when all Danny wanted was to be left in peace.

Pillow fights were usually great fun, but it was obvious to Danny that this would be a bad-tempered occasion. You couldn't enjoy a good battle if there was real animosity between you. At the same time, Marmalade was right. Danny couldn't simply lie there and ignore it. Charlie would be sure to make straight for him. There was no avoiding it.

"Right!" Danny swung his legs out of bed and stood up. "Lend me your pillow, Ed?" The school pillows were all lightweight foam, but Ed complained that he couldn't sleep properly on them, and had brought his own feather pillow from home. It would be a much more formidable weapon.

"Okay."

"What are you going to do?" asked Marmalade.

Danny swapped pillows with Ed and turned to Marmalade. "I'm going to go out of the window and along to the end. I'll climb back in at the end of the corridor and attack Charlie from behind. If he wants a pillow fight, I'll give him one."

Danny's friends stared at him. "We're not allowed to climb out of the window unless there's a fire and we're trapped," protested Marmalade. "It's dangerous."

"It's only dangerous if you're fooling around," retorted Danny. "There's a parapet to stop you falling off the roof. Anyway, there wouldn't be a fire escape there if it was that dangerous." Marmalade didn't look convinced, but Danny was determined to carry on with his plan. "We're not supposed to have pillow fights either, but that's never stopped us in the past," he added.

"There aren't any windows open at the end of the corridor," Ed told him. "How will you get back in?"

"I'll go and open one," offered Ben. He nipped out of their room, and while he was gone, Danny opened the window and looked out.

"You'll get into terrible trouble if you're found out," Ed warned.

A Dreadful Night

But Danny was in no mood to listen. "I've had it up to *here* with Charlie Owen," he said fiercely. "I've *got* to show him that he can't walk all over me."

"I've opened a window just past Charlie's room," Ben told him when he returned. "You should be able to climb in easily and you'll be able to hear him when he comes out of his room to start the fight."

"Thanks."

Danny pushed Ed's large pillow through the bedroom window and clambered out after it. A cold wind was blowing and he wished he'd worn his dressing gown. But in spite of the cold and dark, it really was quite safe to walk along between the bedroom windows and the stone parapet. You would have to be stupid enough to climb up on top of the parapet to have any chance of falling. But being on the roof was strictly against the rules and he *would* get into serious trouble if he were caught.

It only took a few moments to get to the window Ben had opened for him. Danny put his head in and listened. All was quiet. He didn't want to climb in before Charlie and his friends left their room. He wanted to attack from behind, where Charlie would least expect Danny to be.

As he waited, he heard the squeal of a door handle. Charlie's bedroom door must be opening. Danny ducked back out of sight and waited for the four boys to leave their room. He waited a few more seconds to be sure, and then struggled as quietly as he could into the dimly lit corridor.

This was it. But he must hurry. They were already out of sight round the corner, and must almost be at his room by now. He wanted to attack Charlie before anyone else joined in the fight. This was between Danny and Charlie Owen, and Danny meant to give his enemy a nasty surprise.

He gripped the pillow tightly.

I'm going to get you Charlie Owen!

He raised the pillow over his shoulder and started to run, his head down. *Nothing* could stop him now. He was angrier than he'd ever been in his entire life. The injustice of Charlie's behaviour burned in him. The pillow was behind his head, gripped tightly, swung back for maximum effect.

Danny was at full tilt. He sped round the corner. It was too late to stop, even though something about the figure in front of him didn't look quite right. The pillow was already flying through the air and the target was totally unaware of his fate.

Smack! Feathers flew everywhere.

Danny's victim staggered against the wall. His glasses went flying and in the confusion were crunched underfoot. Danny stared, aghast. Charlie didn't wear glasses. Charlie didn't have grey hair or wear a cardigan. This wasn't Charlie. It wasn't even a student. It was the person Danny had hoped to impress until his drum kit had collapsed. It was Mr. Timms!

10 What a Terrible Mistake

It was deathly quiet. Feathers drifted through the air and fell slowly to the floor. Carefully, Mr. Timms bent to pick up his broken glasses. He looked at them closely for a moment and then put them in the pocket of his cardigan.

What was Mr. Timms doing here? He must have taken over from Mr. South for the evening. What bad luck that he'd decided to check up on everyone just now.

Danny wanted to run away, to pretend it hadn't been him. But it was much too late for that. Besides, Mr. Timms knew him very well. And Danny liked Mr. Timms a lot. But that wouldn't help him now. Mr. Timms was

What a Terrible Mistake

probably the worst person he could have done this to in the whole school, except for Mrs. Sharkey, the Principal. He was an excellent engineer and a good teacher, but he didn't make many allowances for youth.

If Danny had bopped Mr. South, it would have been bad enough, but Mr. South had sons of his own and would have understood.

"I'm so sorry, Mr. Timms," said Danny. "I'm really sorry. I didn't realize it was you." Danny picked up a bit of broken lens and handed it to him.

"Is everyone else in your room?" asked Mr. Timms, his voice trembling slightly.

Danny nodded dumbly.

Mr. Timms opened the door to Danny's room. The light was off and everyone seemed to be asleep. "Go to bed then," he said.

Danny went into his room, and the door closed behind him. He was shaking. He got into bed and listened. For a few moments there was silence outside the room. Then he heard footsteps begin to recede down the corridor.

Rivals!

What had happened to Charlie? It couldn't have been him Danny had heard coming out of his room. It must have been Mr. Timms looking *in*, to check that all was well. Charlie and his friends must still be safely tucked up in bed. They wouldn't instigate a pillow fight now, knowing Mr. Timms was on the prowl. What terrible, dreadful bad luck.

Now, Danny could hear the other beds creaking, as his friends sat up.

"What's happened?" whispered Marmalade hoarsely. "Who were you talking to?"

Danny took a deep breath, and tried to steady his voice. "Mr. Timms," he said.

"Mr. Timms?" Marmalade sounded shocked.

"He's on duty, so the pillow fight's off," Danny explained, choking back a sob at the enormity of what he had done.

"Is that what Charlie said?" asked Ed.

"I didn't see him," Danny muttered.

"You didn't get caught climbing in the window, did you?" Ben asked anxiously.

What a Terrible Mistake

"No," Danny told him in a wobbly voice, desperate to be left alone in his misery. "Can you all shut up now?" he begged. "I want to go to sleep."

"I was only asking," objected Ben. Danny didn't reply. He lay down, turned over, closed his eyes and tried to banish the image of the pillow connecting with Mr. Timms's head.

"Are you okay?" asked Marmalade.

Tears squeezed out from under Danny's eyelids as he lay in the dark. With great effort he managed a brief: "Yes". The room fell silent. Danny wiped his eyes with his hand and hunched under his duvet. This had to be the worst night of his entire life.

In the morning, Danny woke long before the others. He'd hardly slept. His mind had relived what he'd done, over and over again. Now he felt hollow inside. He knew he must surely be in line to be expelled from school. His worries about trying to get Charlie to practise with him had been swept away by this new, appalling disaster.

Rivals!

Danny got up quietly and went downstairs. He opened the front door and stood for a moment on the doorstep. He looked out and shivered. It was still dark and there was frost on the path. It was going to be a very cold day, but it wasn't the cold that made his heart ache.

He wanted to put on his coat and run away, but he forced himself to close the door again. Danny wasn't a quitter. And he knew that running away wouldn't solve anything. So instead he went along the corridor and rang Mr. South's doorbell. The housemaster was having breakfast.

"Whatever's the matter?" he said, seeing Danny's pinched and pale face. "You'd better come in."

Danny told him everything. Things had gone much too far now for him to be able to cope on his own. Mr. South listened as he ate his toast, and he grew more and more serious as the whole sorry tale emerged.

"Why on earth didn't you come to me as soon as Charlie started behaving badly?" he asked angrily. "You know bullying isn't acceptable at this school. But it'll never be stopped if people don't complain. Now things have really got out of hand. I wish I hadn't gone off duty early last night," he added. "If I'd been here I could have prevented this mess from ever happening. But I can't be on duty twenty-four hours a day."

Danny didn't know what to say, so he shook his head slightly.

Mr. South got up and took his empty cereal bowl and plate to the sink. "Well, it's too late now. Questions will be asked, Mrs. Sharkey will be involved, and you do realize, don't you, that Mr. Timms could ask for you to be expelled? I'll do what I can to help you, but it may not be enough. You of *all* people, Danny. What a waste. I can't believe it. Assaulting a member of staff is never acceptable, no matter what the excuse."

"I know." Danny took a deep, wobbly breath. "I'd like to go and see Mr. Timms, to apologize again. Would that be all right?"

Mr. South sighed. "I don't know, Danny. It might be better to leave it for the moment. I'll phone him and make sure he knows how badly you feel, and tell him the circumstances behind what happened. Let's see what sort of mood he's in before you see him again."

Then the telephone rang and Mr. South went to answer it. When he came back, he was looking grave.

"That was the Principal," he told Danny. "She wants to see you right away."

Much later, Danny appeared in the dining room for a late breakfast. He got a glass of milk and went to sit by himself. He looked small, hunched up and very alone.

Ed and Chloe looked at Marmalade.

"Why hasn't he come over to us?" asked Chloe.

"We ought to go and make sure he's okay," said Ed uneasily.

"He's obviously not okay," said Marmalade. "Something awful must have happened last night. And where did he get to this morning?"

Mr. South had lectured all the boys in the house before breakfast. He hadn't mentioned Danny, but he'd made it very clear that pillow fights were not to be tolerated in future. Everyone had been buzzing with questions, wondering what had caused the lecture and where Danny had got to, but Mr. South hadn't been forthcoming.

"I'll go and sit with him," Marmalade announced. "You lot stay here." He went over to Danny's table and sat down. Danny glanced at him and then away again. It was obvious he didn't want to talk.

"Danny? Come on. I'm your best mate. What's the matter? Where have you been? You can tell me. I might be able to help."

Danny sipped his milk and then pushed it away from him. His stomach was churning and he couldn't force himself to drink it. And his best friend was sitting beside him, wanting to help, but Danny couldn't make himself confide, even in Marmalade.

"I can't," he said, turning to his friend at last, too overwhelmed by what had happened even to begin to explain. "I'm sorry, Marmalade. I just can't."

11 A Difficult Time

But Danny badly needed to confide in someone. And after a few minutes, all his friends had gathered round sympathetically. They might not know what was wrong, but they were unanimous in wanting to help.

Chloe sat down next to Danny and put her hand on his arm. "Is it something else that Charlie has done?" she asked gently.

Danny shook his head.

"Is it something Mr. Timms said last night to upset you?" Marmalade tried to guess, but Danny shook his head again.

"No!" he told them.

"*What* then?" asked Chloe, at a loss.

A Difficult Time

"It's not *them,*" Danny burst out. "It's *me.*" He buried his head in his hands and groaned. "It's what *I* did that's so terrible. I...I hit Mr. Timms instead of Charlie."

There was a stunned silence.

"I didn't do it on *purpose!*" Danny added roughly, looking up again. "I...I was all ready to hit Charlie with the pillow. I raced round the corner to get him. I was *sure* it would be him there. Then...by the time I realized it wasn't...it was too late."

No one knew what to say.

"I've just been to see Mrs. Sharkey," Danny added in a small voice.

"What did she say?" asked Marmalade anxiously.

Danny took a deep, shuddering breath. "I thought I was going to be expelled," he said shakily. "Maybe I would have been if I hadn't got on so well with Mr. Timms in the past. Mrs. Sharkey made it clear that it was Mr. Timms who was giving me a second chance." He looked at his hands. "It was him who decided my punishment too," he added.

Marmalade gripped Danny's shoulder. "I'm sorry,"

he said. "If I hadn't mentioned the pillow fight none of this would have happened."

"It's not your fault," Danny told him. "And I'll get through this, though it's not going to be easy. I had little enough free time before, but now I have to keep the studio tidy and assist Mr. Timms when he wants me. As well as that, I'm not allowed to use the studio myself for the rest of the term. I was going to record Charlie's part of *Conversation Piece* so I could play along to the tape and get the timings right, but now I can't."

Marmalade shook his head. "That's not good," he agreed.

"No. And I'm not going to have much time to practise *anything* for the concert now, but at least I haven't been expelled." He tried to smile, but the smile went wrong and he gulped to stop himself from crying.

"We'll all help," offered Chloe. "And if we spread the word, I'm sure most people will make more of an effort to tidy away properly. They're supposed to, anyway."

Ed looked at the clock. "We ought to get going or we'll be late for our first lesson," he said reluctantly.

A Difficult Time

"I can't even remember what lesson it is," said Danny, rubbing his hands over his tired, prickling eyes.

"Geography first. Then we're in the recording studio for a single lesson," Chloe offered.

Danny groaned. He wasn't sure he could face Mr. Timms again, so soon after seeing him in Mrs. Sharkey's office.

But it was all right. Mr. Timms made no reference to Danny's disgrace and most people were too interested in the lesson to notice Danny's red-rimmed eyes and pale face, or that Mr. Timms was wearing different glasses.

"This is called a Neumann microphone," Mr. Timms told the class. "You can buy cheaper mics, but this is the standard used for vocals. See how it's suspended by elastic on the stand."

"Why?" asked Chloe, who was keen to know all she could about anything to do with singing.

"When we make a recording we don't want any outside noise to spoil it," Mr. Timms said. "Even vibration through the floor can make a difference, but if the mic is suspended from the stand by elastic it won't pick up the vibration, and the recording will be purer. After all, a voice is vibration too, and we only want to pick up the sounds it makes, nothing else. And what about this fabric, stretched in front of the mic? What do you think that's for?"

"Is it to make the sounds softer?" asked Pop, another keen singer.

"Nearly," Mr. Timms told her. "The hard, popping sounds we make, like *t, p* or *ch* can sound like explosions when picked up by such a delicate piece of equipment. The fabric baffle not only mutes the explosive sounds a little, it also protects the mic from any spit."

"Ugh!" said someone from the back. Mr. Timms looked up in annoyance and Danny was relieved it wasn't him in trouble this time.

"A fine gold membrane is stretched inside the mic, which is another reason this piece of equipment is expensive and needs protecting," he said. He picked up a pile of papers and held them out.

A Difficult Time

"These worksheets contain more information about microphones and how they work. For your homework, read them carefully and answer the questions. Don't push!" he added, as everyone surged forward to take one. "Mind the mic!"

In the days that followed, Danny became very familiar with the way Mr. Timms liked things done. He was quite a perfectionist and had a method for everything, from coiling cables, to setting sound levels. He liked his studio kept scrupulously tidy. Danny's presence there was supposed to be a punishment, and it certainly ate seriously into his free time. But apart from fretting about Charlie's continuing refusal to cooperate on *Conversation Piece,* Danny found he was enjoying spending so much time with Mr. Timms.

Being in the studio so much also kept him well out of Charlie's way, and Danny realized too that Mr. South must have said something to make Charlie back off, because he didn't seem quite so keen to bait Danny when they were together.

Rivals!

Fortunately, Mr. Timms wasn't one to bear a grudge and he already knew how genuine Danny's interest was in his subject.

"You see, she was singing a bit flat here," Mr. Timms told him one evening when they were mixing a recording made earlier in the day. "But when I put the sound through this box I can distort the note until it's right."

Danny listened. With a flick of a switch Mr. Timms wobbled the girl's voice with the auto tune, until it was spot on.

"It's far better if they can sing every note perfectly in the first place," Mr. Timms told Danny. "But this is useful if the rest of a recording is excellent and you just need to tweak the odd note."

"Isn't it...well, cheating?" asked Danny.

Mr. Timms nodded. "You could say that," he agreed. "But nowadays a studio recording isn't supposed to be like a live performance. In a real performance, of course you're going to get the odd mistake, but you also get a sense of the musician's excitement and energy at being onstage. In the studio, you're looking for perfection. Don't forget, every live performance is unique, but you're going to be listening to a CD time after time."

"I suppose mistakes would become irritating if you heard them over and over again," admitted Danny.

"That's right," Mr. Timms agreed.

"I'll wash up our mugs," Danny offered at the end of the evening. He was rewarded by a nod and a slight smile from Mr. Timms.

It was homework time and Marmalade and Ed had come to fetch Danny from the studio.

"I'm actually enjoying myself," Danny admitted with a grin as he drained the sink and dried his hands. "If I wasn't so determined to be a drummer, I might even want to be a recording engineer. This studio is great!"

They made their way over to their boarding house and went into the homework room. Charlie was there with Harry.

"I don't know why you don't take your bed to the studio," Harry said. "You're always over there, slaving for Mr. Timms."

Rivals!

"He's teaching me a lot," Danny retorted. "More than you'll ever learn, I bet."

Charlie looked angry. "Some punishment," he snapped. "Trust you to con Timms into thinking you're the best thing since digital recording!"

Danny shrugged and turned away. He wished he hadn't said anything now. Perhaps Charlie would try to make trouble for him again. With the concert fast approaching, he couldn't afford anything else to go wrong.

12 Brought to Account

A few days before the concert, Danny and Chloe were walking down the corridor together when they met Charlie round a corner. To Chloe's amazement, Danny spoke to him cheerfully.

"Hey, fancy a run-through of our piece this afternoon?" he asked. Charlie looked as surprised as Chloe felt.

"What time?" he asked.

"I can only do it at six," Danny said.

A slow smile crept over Charlie's face. "Nah," he said. "I'm not practising then. *The Simpsons* is on, you sad act."

Charlie brushed past and carried on. Chloe turned

to watch him go. When she turned back to Danny, she almost collided with Judge Jim Henson.

"Charlie!" Judge Jim's voice was mild but his eyes showed how angry he was. He must have heard the whole thing.

Charlie came back, keeping his expression neutral.

"Favourite TV shows can wait," Judge Jim told him. "Be in the Rock Department main room with your drums at six. You can cart *your* kit around, as you're bein' so difficult. Besides, a practice room will be too small for two drum kits. Danny can use the department's own kit. And don't even think of not turning up," he added coldly. "I shall be in my office and will be able to hear what you're doing."

"Okay," Charlie mumbled, shooting Danny a venomous look before he sidled off.

"That was lucky," Chloe said to Danny after Judge Jim had gone too.

"It wasn't lucky at all," Danny replied. It was the first time Chloe had seen him smile for ages. "I noticed Judge Jim coming out of the practice room behind

Charlie and hoped he'd overhear our conversation."

"You sneaky thing!" Chloe squeaked. "I didn't realize you could be so devious."

"It wasn't planned," he told her seriously. "I really *did* want to ask Charlie about a practice. We need at least one run-through together, to get the timings right. But I sort of assumed he wouldn't want to. When I saw Judge Jim coming along, I thought it was a good opportunity to get him to agree."

"I bet Charlie would have said yes straight away if he'd realized he was being overheard," said Chloe with a grin. "You really dropped him in it."

"He's stupid," Danny said. "We badly need to practise this piece together. Otherwise it'll be a pretty awful performance. With Charlie's attitude, *Conversation Piece* is going to be less like a conversation and more like an argument."

"Never mind," said Chloe. "Everyone will realize you're doing your best with your bit."

"That's all very well," Danny replied soberly. "But if I'm not careful, doing my best with my own part will show Charlie up and make him even more of an enemy."

The run-through in the Rock Department showed Danny how much work *Conversation Piece* needed if it was ever going to sound any good. Charlie had obviously worked on it, but although he started off playing sensibly, very soon he was being as obstructive as possible.

Danny kept hoping Judge Jim would intervene, but he didn't come in until they'd almost finished.

"What matters most?" he asked them both as Charlie started packing up his drums. "Giving a good performance or scoring points?"

Danny was so frustrated by Charlie's lack of cooperation he was fit to burst. But he didn't want to start an argument now, so he said nothing and Charlie simply hung his head. Danny had to rush over to the studio, to mic up a drum kit for Judge Jim, who had a band coming in to record a new song. Even when he arrived at the studio out of breath, Danny was still very angry with Charlie.

Brought to Account

He took the leads out of the cupboard, where they were neatly coiled, and began attaching the drum microphones to the kit. Slowly, he began to relax and forget his troubles as he concentrated on the work in hand.

At first, when Danny heard the door opening he didn't look up. It would be Mr. Timms, or maybe Judge Jim, pleased to see that Danny had got there ahead of them and was working well. So when he did pause and glance up, he was surprised and concerned to see Charlie Owen with a self-satisfied smirk on his face, holding several leads in one hand.

"What are you doing here?" asked Danny warily.

"Thought you might need these," Charlie said. He let several of the leads drop to the floor and kicked them about.

"Don't," Danny told him. "Mr. Timms will be here in a minute."

"No, he won't," Charlie told him smugly. "I saw him heading towards the Rock Department. You can't catch me out like that!" He started walking round Danny and the drum kit, paying out a long lead as he did so.

"This studio is a bit messy," he taunted Danny. "Aren't you supposed to keep it tidy?"

Danny gritted his teeth. He would not allow himself to lose his temper with Charlie. When he did, things always got worse. "Shall we practise again tomorrow?" he asked, trying to deflect Charlie from making any more of a mess.

"I don't need to!" bragged Charlie. "I'll be fine. Of course, I've recorded myself playing your part so I can get the timings right. Pity you can't do that because you're not allowed to use the studio," he added.

"We really should have another run-through before the concert," Danny told him.

"No way," Charlie said, paying out more lead while he wandered round the studio. "If you're such a brilliant drummer, surely you can wait until the performance?"

"You're an idiot," Danny shouted, unable to restrain himself any longer. "You're ruining everything. And stop messing about with those leads!"

Brought to Account

Charlie leered at him. "Scared of Timms getting an ickle bit cross, are you?" Then he threw a loop of cable, hitting a microphone which fell to the floor with a clatter.

"Stop it! This is expensive equipment you're mucking about with," said Danny, picking up the microphone anxiously.

But Charlie wasn't listening. He had taken a coil of lead and was whirling it round his head like a lasso. "Bet I can get this over your head!" he yelled. He slackened his hold slightly and the loop got bigger.

"Charlie! Stop!" called Danny, seriously concerned for all the equipment as well as himself. He stood up and tried to move away from the drum kit, but Charlie kept the loop of lead whirling towards him. It whistled through the air dangerously and Danny became more and more alarmed. Goodness knows what Charlie would try next, if he managed to throw the lead over Danny's head.

Charlie tossed the lead, but Danny ducked, and it hit his shoulder and fell to the ground, narrowly missing the drum kit.

Rivals!

"You idiot!" he shouted at Charlie. "This isn't my drum kit!"

"It's your responsibility though, isn't it?" Charlie laughed. "And drum kits do seem to fall down when you're in charge. You shouldn't leave them over breaktime. Loads of stuff can go wrong with them."

"I knew that was you!" Danny burst out furiously.

"And you didn't even notice I'd unscrewed everything until you started playing," crowed Charlie. "It was a brilliant laugh."

Charlie pulled the lead back and set it whirling again.

"Got you!" he yelled, throwing the lead once more.

To Danny's horror, the lead went badly astray. Instead of lassoing him, it fell short and knocked into the expensive Neumann microphone.

Then, everything happened at once. The mic rocked wildly on its stand. Danny leaped to save it from falling. But as he stretched to catch it, Mr. Timms burst into the room, his face like thunder.

13 Concert Time

"What are you doing?" Mr. Timms yelled as Danny grabbed the microphone stand to stop it falling over.

And another voice was speaking too, coming through the studio speaker from the control room.

"Stop right now!" It was Judge Jim. Danny looked into the control room and could see fury written all over the usually laid-back teacher's face.

Danny gently steadied the stand with his shaking hand and released it. The delicate microphone had been badly knocked by Charlie's throw. It hung at an awkward angle from the elastic cradle. Danny's heart turned over and it was all he could do not to sit down and weep. Once again, it would look as if he was in the wrong, while Charlie got away scot-free. Surely, this time there would be no escaping expulsion from Rockley Park School.

But neither Judge Jim nor Mr. Timms were looking at Danny. Their anger was vented at Charlie Owen.

"Such wilful vandalism will be severely punished," Judge Jim's furious voice told Charlie. "And for a start I'll be writing to your father. Come into the control room."

Charlie obeyed at once, his face ashen.

"Your behaviour has been appalling this term," Judge Jim said to Charlie, his voice still coming clearly through the studio microphone. "All this..." He waved his hand towards the chaotic studio. "...And tampering with Danny's drum kit before a performance. It's totally inexcusable. Unluckily for you, the microphones are turned on and we heard the whole thing. If I could, I'd have you thrown out of Rockley Park this very moment. Go to my office and wait for me there."

Once Charlie had gone, Judge Jim came through to Mr. Timms and Danny. "Is it okay?" he asked Mr. Timms, who was attending to the stricken microphone.

"Hopefully," Mr. Timms replied. "I'll test it when I've got it back in its cradle."

Then Judge Jim turned to Danny. "From what Mr. Timms and I have overheard, I don't think any of this was your fault, Danny," he said. "I had hoped that if you and Charlie played together at the concert, your love of making music would take over and this stupid rivalry would end. But I was wrong."

Judge Jim looked tired, and almost defeated.

"It's all right," he added gently, seeing Danny's worried face. "I know you were willing to give it a go, but I can see it's not going to work. You don't have to play with Charlie Owen."

On the morning of the concert Danny woke early. He lay peacefully in bed for a moment, listening to the central heating coming on. The radiator near his bed was making a ticking sound as it warmed up. Still half asleep, he echoed the ticks with his fingers on the duvet. He took up the sound and ran with it, adding a mixture of beats to complement the radiator's rhythm.

Rivals!

At last he abandoned his almost silent drumming and yawned. He swung his legs out of bed and got up quietly so he wouldn't disturb the others.

Lessons were always cancelled on concert days, and Mr. Timms had released him from his studio duties too, so Danny was free to practise as much as he wanted. Now he was awake he couldn't wait to get to work, so he showered quickly and ran downstairs.

A few other students were about, but most wouldn't surface until a bit later. Danny found himself walking towards the practice rooms in the company of Tony Jackson, a senior drummer.

"You're playing that experimental piece for the junior dancers, aren't you?" he asked.

"Yes," nodded Danny shyly.

"I'm looking forward to hearing that," the boy said. "Hope it goes well for you." He opened the door of the first room and closed it behind him. Danny looked after him admiringly.

Tony Jackson wished me luck! Danny told himself. *Wow!*

Concert Time

It was a good start to the day. Tony Jackson was a jazz drummer and was going on to music college. He was seriously talented, even by Rockley Park standards, and already played with a professional band.

Danny went into his practice room and settled himself behind his drum kit. *Well. Last effort*, he told himself. *All I can do is my best*.

In spite of all the problems, and Judge Jim telling him that he didn't have to, Danny had insisted he wanted to play *Conversation Piece* with Charlie.

Marmalade and the others had told him he was crazy. Hadn't he hated the idea? Hadn't Charlie given him constant grief? Why would he want to play with someone who'd brought him so much trouble?

Danny wasn't sure what made him quite so stubborn. But he'd never liked giving up on anything. And he knew Charlie was a talented drummer. It infuriated him that he could be prepared to spoil the very thing he was best at, for the sake of a bit of jealousy. Surely the joy of playing would take over eventually? But that was what Judge Jim had hoped and it hadn't happened.

Rivals!

Since Charlie daren't refuse to cooperate with Danny any more, practice together had been easier to arrange, but Judge Jim warned Danny that cooperation was no guarantee of good music.

"You can drag him to play," he'd said. "But you can't force his drumming to fly, and that's what you really need. No one will think the worse of you if you pull out."

But Danny hadn't pulled out, and the day of the concert had dawned without him making any headway with Charlie at all.

Danny ran his fingers lightly over all his drums and cymbals. It didn't do to think of Charlie now. He had to run through his other pieces as well. He flexed his shoulders and made a start.

Hunger made him stop eventually, and Danny went to find some breakfast, well pleased with his morning's work. No one was taking leisurely breakfasts this morning. Students ate quickly and rushed off to put the finishing touches to their performances. Marmalade had already eaten and gone back to the dance studio. Chloe, Pop and Lolly were collaborating on one song and had gone back to their room to finalize what to wear. Ed and Ben were busy putting the finishing touches to an acoustic guitar duet they'd been working on. Only Tara was still eating. Danny stopped for a moment to ask her how she was doing.

"I still feel bad I can't play with you, Tara," he said. "How's it going with Charlie?"

Tara gave Danny a wry look. "He's been much better recently."

"He's a good drummer really," Danny said. "When he puts his mind to it."

"Yes, he is." Tara got up to go and then changed her mind. "Danny?"

"What?"

"The other day, Charlie asked me what I do after I've fallen out with someone."

Danny was surprised. "Did he? What did you say?" he asked.

"Not much really," Tara admitted. "It took me by surprise. Charlie's usually so full of himself, but he sounded as if he really wanted to know. I think he regrets acting the way he did, but he doesn't know how to back down."

"Well, I can't do it for him."

"I know that." Tara hesitated. "I thought you ought to know. That's all. See you later."

There was something about concert days that made everyone act differently. Tara was usually prickly and difficult to get on with, and here she was trying to build bridges between him and Charlie.

Well, if he wants to make up, he knows where to find me, thought Danny as he went to collect his drums from the practice room to take them into the theatre.

The door to Tony Jackson's practice room was propped open. Danny could see that he was taking his kit down too.

"Tell you what," he said, noticing Danny. "You can use my kit if you like."

Danny stared at Tony. "Really?" Most musicians were very protective of their instruments and hated anyone else touching them, let alone playing them.

"Yeah! I'm playing three pieces and so are you. It

makes sense to share...and I think my kit is probably a bit better!"

Danny nodded. That was certainly true. "Are you sure?"

Tony laughed. "Course! I wouldn't have offered otherwise. It'll be ideal for Rosie's music." He stopped and drummed his fingers lightly on his snare drum. "Hmm. You might want to use your snare drum instead of mine when you play your stuff, and maybe take a couple more cymbals along, as you play rock rather than jazz. Other than that, you should be fine. I know you'll play it properly, even when you're rocking," he added as Danny continued to look dumbfounded. "You're the business. Everyone knows it."

Danny blushed with pleasure. "Thanks very much!" he said quickly.

"You'll have to pay for it mind," Tony added. Danny's spirits drooped. At this stage in the term, he couldn't even afford a chocolate bar. "I mean by helping me carry it over to the theatre!" Tony said.

"Oh! Right."

Rivals!

Tony grinned at Danny. "Go and fetch your favourite cymbals then, before I break this down, and we'll see which ones sound best with my kit."

It was the sort of day when students cooperated a lot, but still, several people raised their eyebrows to see Tony Jackson allowing a junior student to handle his drums, even if that student was Danny James.

"No one will dare to mess this kit up," Tony said, as they reassembled it in the theatre.

"I hope not!" said Danny, suddenly afraid.

"I *know* not," Tony told him grimly. "I've already had a word with Charlie Owen. Well," he added, laughing at Danny's astonished face, "I want to hear Rosie's piece played properly, without any accidents!"

Danny blushed. He hadn't realized the disaster with his sabotaged drum kit was so widely known.

Judge Jim was onstage, organizing everything. He nodded approvingly when he saw Tony and Danny together.

"That will save a lot of swappin' around during the concert," he said. "Well done."

Concert Time

The audience of teachers, parents and students who were not performing until later was already filing into the theatre when Danny realized he'd forgotten his drumming gloves.

"I must get them," he told Marmalade, who was warming up. "Otherwise I'm bound to get blisters!" He turned to go and almost collided with Charlie. They glanced awkwardly at each other.

"Why are you playing Tony Jackson's kit?" Charlie blurted out.

Danny shrugged and looked at Charlie properly. "Because he offered," he said. "Why? Is there a problem?"

Charlie shook his head. "No," he mumbled uncertainly. "Well...no."

"I've got to get something," Danny told him. "I need to hurry before the concert starts. Sorry."

Danny raced to his room, grabbed his gloves and hurried back. There were only a couple of minutes to go before he was to play his solo, which was the first act of the concert.

Rivals!

Back at the side of the stage, Danny breathed deeply a few times to settle himself. As always before a performance, he was strung up and nervous, but once he sat down behind his drums he was fine.

Today, although he played his solo well, part of his mind was elsewhere. More than anything, he didn't want to let Rosie and the dancers down.

His took his bow to warm applause after his solo, and left the stage. There were several acts to watch before he was needed again, but he couldn't concentrate on any of them. He had to get those rim shots right for the dancers.

Then it was time, and he escorted Rosie onstage for the dancers' big moment.

The theatre went quiet as Marmalade and the rest of the dancers took their places. They were all dressed in ragged clothes, with most wearing various elements of army gear. The African child soldier theme was a very powerful one, and the Art Department had done well with the set. The auditorium was dark, but the stage was brightly lit, with the silhouette of a thorn tree against a bleak, sandy background to suggest the African bush.

The piano and drum kit were off to one side of the stage, so that the dancers had plenty of room. Rosie sat at her piano and nodded at Danny to begin. This time the kit was fine, and Danny gave the piece his best. When it came to the rim shots, he held his nerve. The timing from both dancer and musician was perfect, and Marmalade dropped dead to the floor as if the rim shots really were rifle fire.

The applause at the end was terrific. Rosie grinned triumphantly at Danny, and Marmalade gave him the thumbs up as he went to take his bow with the rest of the dancers. Danny wiped the sweat from his eyes, pleased and relieved. Two performances were done. But still, the most difficult one was yet to come.

14 Danny and Charlie Fight it Out

Danny tried to relax, as he watched the rest of the students, but nothing could stop him worrying about his final performance. Even Chloe's amazing voice failed to distract him, and all too soon it was time for *Conversation Piece*.

A murmur of expectation went through the audience as a second drum kit was moved onto the other side of the stage. A drumming duet was unusual, and word had got around that Danny and Charlie had been feuding, so everyone was curious to see this, the last performance of the day.

Judge Jim had wished everyone luck at the beginning of the concert, but Danny had overheard him say something extra to Charlie.

"Forget your differences, Charlie, and just play," he told him gruffly.

Danny hadn't been able to see his rival's expression. Would Charlie be able to do as Judge Jim had told him? Danny didn't hold out a lot of hope.

As they'd rehearsed it, the two boys were supposed to go on at the same time, from opposite sides of the stage. Danny was in his place, but where was Charlie?

The longer Danny had to wait the more unsettled he felt. Would Charlie totally refuse to go onstage? But perhaps that would serve Danny right. Was it arrogance that had made him so determined to play, in spite of Judge Jim giving him a way out?

He felt so helpless waiting for Charlie to arrive. Then, just when Danny was ready to give up, two spotlights came on, one shining on each kit.

Thank goodness for that! The lights were the cue he needed. Danny took a deep breath and stepped onstage. From the other side, to Danny's relief, Charlie did the same and the audience began to clap.

Rivals!

Both boys sat down. Charlie readjusted his seat.

"Well," Danny muttered to himself. "This is it." He ran his fingers gently over each drum and cymbal, as he always did, and the instruments whispered back to him. When he was ready he sat quietly on his stool, sticks ready, waiting for Charlie.

Charlie took ages and by the time he picked up his sticks some kids in the audience were getting restless, and Danny's whole body was tense.

Charlie had to start off, so Danny watched his enemy closely in case he tried to start without warning. But Charlie was behaving for once. He nodded slightly to his rival, raised his sticks, and began.

The opening was a furious crash on the cymbals. After that, Charlie got started on his drums.

It was supposed to be a conversation. Charlie was supposed to play a phrase and then wait for Danny to echo it before he went on to the next phrase. But it was obvious he hadn't managed to put all his resentment behind him. He wasn't letting Danny finish *his* part before he started the next. It happened over and over again, although Danny quickened his pace to try and get his phrases in.

Danny felt a slow flush of anger spreading through him and tried to keep calm. Charlie's timing wasn't *that* bad. He was deliberately trying to make Danny look stupid. But anger wouldn't help Danny to sort this out.

Come on Charlie. Don't be a idiot! thought Danny. Charlie's playing was spoiling the piece *and* making Danny sound as if he wasn't properly prepared. He had to do something. He simply couldn't let Charlie stay in control.

All of a sudden, Danny burst into a furious tirade of blows on his drums. He went round the whole kit, thrashing his toms, the snare drum, all the cymbals and keeping up a deep insistent thud on the bass drum. Before Charlie could recover Danny had taken over the lead and was playing the next phrase. He played it while keeping the bass rhythm going extra loud, as if to press home the fact that this was the way the timing should be. Charlie replied, but his timing

Rivals!

was out and his sticks hesitant, as if he didn't know what was going on.

Danny played the next phrase and Charlie replied, but it was a struggle, as if he were fighting the piece. His resentment must be obvious to everybody. Now he was playing over Danny again, rushing the pace, trying to take over once more.

Danny kept his head and played doggedly on, keeping faith with the piece, but giving nothing away to his enemy. Now he'd got the upper hand he was determined not to lose it.

Come on! he silently urged himself and his adversary. *Get your drums talking! And play properly! Beat for beat!*

It was no use. The piece should have ended with both sets of drums playing in harmony, but Charlie was still determined to spoil things, even at the end. In spite of everything Danny could do, the climax was ragged instead of crisp and the audience was unimpressed. A ripple of applause was all the boys were going to get for this performance.

Danny and Charlie Fight it Out

They both bowed briefly where they were sitting. Then Charlie was getting up from his kit, but Danny stayed where he was. Charlie hadn't managed to make him look quite like an idiot, but nothing had been resolved between them. This whole term had been spoiled by Charlie's behaviour. Danny couldn't just leave it at that. They had to settle their differences once and for all.

I don't want a rival. I want to drum! he thought angrily.

His frustration boiled over, and before he could stop himself he let out a furious series of challenging rim shots. They were played impeccably, beats like rifle fire, even more shocking than when he'd played them for the dancers.

Charlie hesitated.

Judge Jim Henson was down at the front of the audience. Danny had noticed him stand up with a resigned expression on his face. Now he was sitting down again, watching the two boys keenly.

Danny fired off two more rim shots. They were followed by total silence in the auditorium. The

Rivals!

audience had been getting ready to go but now everyone hesitated, wondering what was going on. Surely the performance was over...or was it?

Danny forgot about the audience. He focused on communicating with Charlie in the way he knew best. He fired off two more shots into the silence. *Blat! Blat!*

It was an unmistakable challenge. But what was Charlie going to do about it? For a moment it looked as if he was going to stalk offstage, leaving Danny unanswered. But when another couple of shots rang out he sat down again. The audience held their breath.

Danny stared at Charlie across the expanse of empty stage and waited. Charlie picked up his sticks. He knew better than to reply with more rim shots. They were much too difficult, and the reason he'd lost out to Danny in the first place. Instead he beat out an insistent rhythm on his tom-toms. Both sticks thudded onto the toms at the same time. *Bam bam! Bam bam! Bam bam!* Danny listened for a moment and picked up the beat on his bass. Now they were locked into the same beat together. It was heavy and dark, almost unbearable in its intensity. Who was going to break out of it first?

Danny again. He attacked his cymbals, and where he led Charlie followed. Danny eased back and let Charlie take over. Charlie splashed all his metal and then kept the pace going on his ride cymbal, out of ideas, watching Danny now, wondering what was going to happen next. Danny hit and pedalled his high hat in answer, changing the mood, with the lovely soft *ksch! tck! ksch! tck!* as the top cymbal closed on the bottom one.

They kept glancing at each other. And the beat was changing. It was in time, pulsing, waiting for the next run of sound.

In turn they added more instruments to the rhythm. Charlie added a floor tom, Danny rattled the snare drum, Charlie hit his crash cymbal and Danny played the ride. The noise was building; it was rising to a heart-stopping, mind-numbing cacophony of sound.

Now they were playing every instrument they had,

their kits yelling to each other across the stage. No one had the upper hand, no one was in charge, but the sound was passionate, with a terrible intensity, and ear-splittingly loud. And it was growing, building to an inevitable climax.

The boys were running with sweat, playing their hearts out. Charlie was doing better than he had for ages. They were beat for beat, the stage jumping with sound. Urging each other on, in harmony at last, Danny gave Charlie the nod for the last shuddering crescendo. They played it in perfect time. Then it was over.

But there wasn't silence for long. The whole audience was cheering and clapping, stamping their feet and waving their arms above their heads. No one had ever seen or heard anything like it.

Both boys were slumped on their stools, their hair dark with sweat and plastered to their heads. For a few seconds they sat where they were, bent with exhaustion. Then Danny raised his head and glanced over at Charlie. As one, both boys stood up. They moved to the centre of the stage and bowed. The audience went wild. Now Danny was holding out his hand and as everyone watched, Charlie slowly reached out and shook it.

Danny wasn't sure how he got offstage. The thunderous applause had carried on, the students drumming their feet with approval until Judge Jim had to come up onstage to calm everyone down. Then the auditorium lights came up and it was all over.

Danny was congratulating Chloe, Pop and Lolly on their great performances when he felt someone at his elbow. It was Charlie.

"That was a fantastic duet!" Chloe enthused to both boys. "Well done!"

Charlie nodded. "Thanks," he said.

Once Chloe had gone he looked at Danny. "Want to swap drumsticks?" he asked. "You know," he added diffidently, "like footballers do with their shirts after a match?"

Danny looked at his sticks. It was a wonder they

hadn't snapped. The head of one stick had sheered half off, and both were so chipped and frayed they were almost useless.

"Well..." He showed Charlie the sticks and shrugged. "If you want them..."

But Charlie was looking anxious. "No, I want to *swap*. Yours for mine. Look."

Charlie was holding out a pair of expensive, Japanese oak sticks that were almost brand new. Danny looked at Charlie, and Charlie nodded.

"Go on. Take them." He blushed, and thrust them at Danny. "Go on. They're for...you know."

"Okay." Danny took them. "Thanks."

Tara pushed her way out of the throng of performers and joined them. "Great duet," she told them enthusiastically. Then she faced Charlie. "I actually enjoyed our performance too," she added. "It was fun. Thanks for playing so well." She put her arms round Charlie and gave him a brief hug.

Charlie's eyes met Danny's and the two boys grinned. Tara wasn't known for her demonstrative nature. The euphoria of the concert must have even rubbed off on her.

When she'd gone, Danny cleared his throat. "Well..."

Charlie shrugged and looked embarrassed. Then he gave a half smile.

"Thanks," he offered. "It was good...in the end." He hesitated. "Wasn't it?"

"Oh, yeah," Danny agreed. "In the end it was *great*! We really flew."

"We should play again sometime," said Charlie.

"Yeah," said Danny with a grin, clutching his new sticks. "I think we should."

So you want to be a pop star?

Turn the page to read some top tips on how to make your dreams come true...

✶ Making it in the music biz ✶

Think you've got tons of talent?
Well, music maestro Judge Jim Henson,
Head of Rock at top talent academy Rockley
Park, has put together his hot tips to help
you become a superstar...

✶ Number One Rule: Be positive!
You've got to believe in yourself.

✶ Be active! Join your school choir
or form your own band.

✶ Be different! Don't be afraid to stand
out from the crowd.

✶ Be determined! Work hard and stay focused.

✶ Be creative! Try writing your own material –
it will say something unique about you.

✶ Be patient! Don't give up if things
don't happen overnight.

✶ Be ready to seize opportunities
when they come along.

✳ Be versatile! Don't have a one-track mind – try out new things and gain as many skills as you can.

✳ Be passionate! Don't be afraid to show some emotion in your performance.

✳ Be sure to watch, listen and learn all the time.

✳ Be willing to help others. You'll learn more that way.

✳ Be smart! Don't neglect your school work.

✳ Be cool and don't get big-headed! Everyone needs friends, so don't leave them behind.

✳ Always stay true to yourself.

✳ And finally, and most importantly, enjoy what you do!

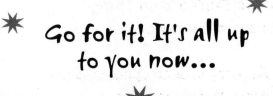

Go for it! It's all up to you now...

Usborne Quicklinks

For links to exciting websites where you can find out more about becoming a pop star and even practise your singing with online karaoke, go to the Usborne Quicklinks Website at www.usborne-quicklinks.com and enter the keywords "fame school".

Internet safety

When using the Internet make sure you follow these safety guidelines:

❋ Ask an adult's permission before using the Internet.

❋ Never give out personal information, such as your name, address or telephone number.

❋ If a website asks you to type in your name or email address, check with an adult first.

❋ If you receive an email from someone you don't know, do not reply to it.

For another fix of

read

Tara's Triumph

1 Alone

Tara stepped out of the shower and put on her last clean shirt. She looked longingly at her freshly made bed, with the mosquito netting neatly furled. But she couldn't go back to bed, even though she'd been up since five a.m., and had just got back from the morning's safari. She had a very long journey ahead of her, and she wasn't looking forward one bit to travelling alone.

She picked up her earphones, and put some music on. She'd filled the player with all her favourite tracks before she'd come on holiday and now she tried to blot out her tiredness with some heavy rock as she began to pack.

The staff at the game lodge had been lovely to her. The owners, Connie and Tambo Sissulu, were old friends of her parents. They had looked after Tara really well and had tried hard to make her feel at home. Jimmy, their safari guide, had been brilliant at including her, sometimes even letting her ride up in front of the safari bus with him. But even seeing the big game animals of Africa hadn't cheered Tara up. She was feeling very let down, and spending the last two days of her holiday with a variety of middle-aged couples, with their baggy shorts and tedious conversation hadn't helped. She was sure that none of them would share her passion for music, and she hadn't mentioned to anyone how much she missed playing her bass guitar.

It wasn't supposed to have been like this. It should have been a family holiday with both her parents. It was going to have been a fantastic week on safari, all three of them together for once. But that's not how it had turned out. Things had gone wrong almost from the start.

"Unfortunately, I shall have to fly back home a

couple of days early," Tara's dad had announced over dinner on the first night. "I've just been asked to step in at the last minute for a really important recording session. They need me in London on Friday, which is two days before the end of our holiday."

"Oh no! Darling. Can't you tell them you won't do it?" protested Tara's mum.

Tara had played with her exotic fruit salad while she listened to her parents' arguing voices drowning out the night sounds of the African bush. They should all be sitting quietly, listening to those fantastic roars and screeches out there in the dark. They should all be excited at being in Africa, not discussing going home already, but Tara's parents' careers got in the way of everything.

"Sorry. No. I can't turn this one down," her father had replied. "But we'll still have five days together."

Tara's father was a jazz musician who was constantly in demand. Her mother was a fashion journalist. They both spent lots of their time jetting around the world at a moment's notice, and now it seemed they couldn't even manage a week together as a family without one of them ruining it.

Tara tried not to be too unhappy at her dad having to leave early. But it turned out that her father wasn't the only person to let her down. Soon her mother had abandoned the family holiday as well.

After three wonderful days, her mother had got wind of an important photo shoot happening on the coast. First there had been constant phone calls, then she had dropped the bombshell.

"I shall have to leave in the morning, and I won't be back for the rest of the week," she had announced to Tara's dismay. "Don't be difficult, darling," she had added, noticing Tara's fallen face. "The rumour is that Tikki Deacon is in Africa for more than just a modelling assignment. You know how famous she is. It could be a really big story. I can't let my editor down, can I?"

So that was Tara's holiday ruined. Three days as a family, two more with her dad, and the last two abandoned by both her parents. Tara bit back the angry words she felt like saying. She didn't want to spoil the last little bit of time they had together. She listened dejectedly while her parents discussed what they should do with their daughter for the final two days of the holiday. Their conversation made Tara feel like a parcel. No one asked her what she thought of the way things had turned out.

"We could send her to my mother," Tara's mum mused, "but then there's the problem of getting Tara back to school, now Mother doesn't drive."

"Do you have a friend you'd like to stay with, sweetie?" asked her dad hopefully. "That would make it easier to get her to school," he added to his wife, ignoring Tara's mumbled reply.

There wasn't anyone Tara wanted to stay with, especially at such short notice. She didn't want anyone feeling sorry for her.

"Can't I fly back with you on Thursday?" she had begged her dad.

But her father had been adamant. "As soon as I get back to London I'll be in the studio, and you know what long hours that means," he told her. "I expect I'll be working through the night. That would be no fun for you, and I couldn't leave you at home for so long on your own either."

"Let's have a word with Connie and Tambo," suggested her mum. "Just because we have to leave, it doesn't mean Tara needs to miss the rest of the safari. I'm sure they'll be fine about keeping an eye on you," she told Tara cheerfully. "You wouldn't want to be dragged from pillar to post with me in this heat, would you? You'll have loads to do here, with two game drives each day, and there's the pool to relax in too."

"If we make sure she can connect straightaway to the London flight she'll be fine," Tara's dad added. "And I'll arrange for a car to pick you up from Heathrow and take you to school," he told Tara. And so that had been that.

Tara hadn't made a fuss, but soon afterwards she went to her room. She put some music on and stared miserably out of the window. If only she had her bass with her. At least music was reliable. It seemed it was the only thing in her life that was. Her parents were far too wrapped up in their careers to notice her real feelings.

Once again, Tara would be turning up at school for a new term without her mum and dad there to give her a hug and wish her all the best. Rockley Park was a boarding school, and all the other parents dropped their children off themselves. Tara hated arriving on her own. It just wasn't fair.

At least Tara enjoyed school. Although it offered all the usual lessons, Rockley Park also taught the students everything they needed to know about making it in the music industry. And Tara had great musical ambitions. She dreamed of belonging to a really successful rock band. One day, she was determined to become far more famous even than her dad. He was a very well respected saxophonist, but most of his work was in the recording studio, accompanying other famous musicians when they made their CDs. Tara wanted to be out there playing her bass on stage, and hearing the cheers of her devoted fans. They would travel across continents to see her, not leave her in the lurch like her parents so often did.

Tara stuffed the few remaining possessions into her bag and lugged it down to reception. Jimmy was waiting for her, his handsome face beaming. Tara gave him the luggage, and thrust her earphones and player into her pocket.

"All ready?" asked Jimmy.

Tara nodded. Connie and Tambo each gave her a big hug, and told her to take care. Tara had the impression that they didn't really approve of the way her parents had abandoned her either.

"You enjoy your new term now," Connie said. "And as soon as you're famous be sure to send me your first CD."

Jimmy and Tara clambered into the lodge's single-engine aeroplane, and strapped themselves in. The small plane was soon bumping and rattling its way over the red earth of the landing strip, and then it was up, and gaining height. Once they reached the city airport, Jimmy was going to hand Tara safely over to the airline chaperone who would be there to take care of her.

They arrived at the bustling terminal, and Jimmy helped Tara check in her bag. Then he made sure she had her passport, boarding card and hand luggage, before seeing her to the boarding gate where her chaperone was waiting. He gave Tara a cheerful smile and a wave, before striding off in search of his next group of tourists.

Tara watched him go. She knew her father would have paid Jimmy well for looking after her, but he had been very kind, and she would miss his bad jokes and fantastic animal stories.

But by the time they landed at Heathrow, Jimmy and Africa seemed a lifetime away. The airline chaperone had irritated Tara intensely by treating her like a child, and the constant drumming of the plane's engines had stopped her from getting any sleep. What with that and her early start, Tara was exhausted. Thank goodness her dad had been as good as his word and had arranged for someone to meet her. As Tara emerged from customs she scanned the mass of expectant faces, and finally spotted a young woman at the barrier who was holding a hurriedly written sign with Tara's name on it.

"Did you have a good flight?" the woman enquired. She didn't wait for an answer, but led the way out to where the car was parked. Tara slumped in the back, and tried to feel happy about returning to school on her own. She ought to be used to it by now.

To find out what happens next read

 Tara's Triumph

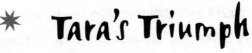

Cindy Jefferies' varied career has included being a Venetian-mask maker and a video DJ. Cindy decided to write *Fame School* after experiencing the ups and downs of her children, who have all been involved in the music business. Her insight into the lives of wannabe pop stars and her own musical background means that Cindy knows how exciting and demanding the quest for fame and fortune can be.

Cindy lives on a farm in Gloucestershire, where the animal noises, roaring tractors and rehearsals of Stitch, her son's indie-rock band, all help her write!

To find out more about Cindy Jefferies, visit her website: www.cindyjefferies.co.uk